When Smoke Rises

Stephanie Tarver

FINEWORKS PUBLISHING

For more information, address: stephanietarverbooks@gmail.com or

fineworkspublishing@gmail.com.

Names: Stephanie Tarver author.

Title: When Smoke Rises: a novel / Stephanie Tarver.

Description: FineWorks Publishing LLC first edition. / Alabama: FineWorks Publishing LLC 2023

Identifiers: LCCN 2024915771

ISBN 979-8-9895439-1-5 (hardcover) / ISBN 979-8-9895439-0-8 (paperback) / ISBN 979-8-9895439-2-2 (epub)

www.stephanietarverbooks.com

To Brian, Virginia, and James

The hearts were heavy,
The souls grew weary.
The hands bared scars
From the loads we carried.
The love we knew,
Was all that we had.
Whispered dreams, and tears we shed.
Through storms and shadows
Our love remained.
Turning burdens to blessings—
we found our way.

When Smoke Rises

Stephanie Tarver

FINEWORKS PUBLISHING

Kitten Smoke Rises

Stephanie Tarver

Fine Words Publishing

A shared flame, weaving a new chapter
of warmth and connection-
Turning the remnants of rising smoke
into the sparks of a vibrant, shared odyssey.
For the shadows of the night befall us-
But she that believes shall rise.
Rise up out of the ashes like smoke,
becoming sparks and embers, electrified.

Acknowledgements

This novel has been a long labor of love, with much prayer and consideration. I dedicate this book to those who have contributed to the motivation and creativity of my writing and to the completion of my work by supporting and encouraging me to keep going, in pursuit of my crown achievement. I hope readers find inspiration, healing, and courage in this novel. Thank you to my family and friends who nurtured my abilities as a professional and celebrated this wonderful opportunity with me. Thank you for your patience and for the solidarity you've expressed as I finally realize my dream of becoming a published author.

"May Your Smoke, Always Rise"

Prologue

In every life resides a narrative, a lengthy suppressed tail, awaiting expression in words yearning to be uttered. Bringing to question, would anyone truly believe that it happened, or better yet, happened to me? A question that I have asked myself a dozen times if not more. I often wondered if I dared to face my fears head-on and make the delivery; to write it. To deliver a heart throbbing, gut-wrenching, bare bones tell all about my life, but did I really want to tell all? Was I truly ready to uncover the secret hidden behind the veil?

I found that individuals could be remarkably cold. Willfully casting judgment just because their journey was different from mine. I found myself living a life shrouded in concealed realities, burdened by an unpleasant truth. Always handed down by those who never walked a single step in my shoes, individuals indifferent to the inner challenges, or the origins thereof. Those who are solely captivated by gossip and speculative allure.

I became acquainted with a life filled with highs and lows; knowing what it's like to be put in a box but also on a pedestal. To endure intense trials and tribulation to a near breaking point. To fear living and face devastation that devoured me from within. Like being trapped in a suffocating darkness, I have been abused, abandoned, and defamed. But among the ashes, I have embraced my battles with a profound and given hope. One that made me believe not only in myself but, ultimately in God. I've found that only He can deliver and provide refuge and strength to the lowly. It is because of Him that I live and thrive and have the strength that I do today. To believe that I am worthy, and to believe in Him, the life giver and the redeemer, the one who saves.

My name is Hope, and this is my story.

Chapter One

With heavy rain pelting the windowpane, my eyelids became weighted, and my body was very still. I couldn't wait for Carl to get home. I was determined to stay awake until he came through the door. It was ten o'clock in the evening and the local news was on when I finally fell asleep. Carl worked late some nights at the furniture store in a nearby city because his previous employer went out of business in our small, poverty-stricken town. Carl adored his job, thriving in his role, and the commute did not seem to bother him much. We entertained the idea of relocating as soon as he could get a transfer. "Texas" he said, was the place for us to have a better life. Carl was convinced we could forge a brighter future far away from Selma.

With a population of about 30,000 people, Selma was rich in history. Nestled along the picturesque Alabama River, boasting a blend of charm and beauty. The town's landscape unfolded like a living canvas, reflecting the vibrant hues of the southern sky while the air imbued of sweet magnolias and towering oaks. The streets echoed with the whispers of an old town adorned with well-preserved architecture and warm hospitality. Known by her moniker "The Queen City," Selma was home to the Civil Rights Movement and, as it was, very monumental in Selma.

There was, of course, the famous bridge where it all happened on Bloody Sunday, a landmark that would never let us forget those who fought for freedom but also a reminder of how far we still had to go for racial harmony. Still, that bridge was more to most folks than just a piece of history. It was a symbolic treasure, and it was home. It was a representation of things past and those present.

Serving as a marker, a tourist attraction, a platform that welcomed countless public officials and government dignitaries. That landmark bore a symbolism of hope, heartache, and tragedy.

People came to our fair city from all over the world just to see it, touch it, and walk the path of foot soldiers from 1965. It stood as a potent and meaningful figuration. A gateway to new avenues and experiences that would forever shape my future. My Arch of Freedom, guiding me towards love, success, and unexpected encounters.

Little did I know that bridge would tragically intersect my life on one unforgettable day in April. A visceral reminder of the fragility of life. A day that would transcend the confines of time for all who loved Carl Fisher.

Carl was a man of thoughtful duty and unyielding determination. Easy on the eyes, he possessed a commanding stature, with features that captured attention wherever he went. He stood tall, amidst his skyline of success and achievements. Yet, beneath the polished veneer of triumph, lay a heart anchored in humility and compassion. His success was not measured by his wealth or accolades, but by the lives he touched, and the positive change he fostered. He was a visionary, harboring ambitions to one day own a prominent furniture franchise. He wanted to elevate his career to the highest level possible.

"Hope, it will be grand! 90,000 square feet of the finest furniture and home décor. The sign will say: Fisher Fine Furnishings." He was a planner. Often envisioning our budding future right down to the smallest detail. "We are going places. Moving on up!" His eyes glistened each time he spoke about it.

There was an undeniable aura of self-assurance that emanated from Carl. He exuded a certain poise and understanding that spoke to his keen perception and contemplation. But what truly set him apart was his knack for reading people and foreseeing potential conflicts. A quality that made him very discerning of whom he invited into his inner circle. "You're only as good as the company you keep." Carl believed in that philosophy, just like he believed in his work. It was his passion. He spent years as an understudy, learning the furniture and retail sales business inside and out.

Starting as a floor sales associate, Carl worked his way up to the position of store manager in just three years. His keen acumen for numbers proved to be an essential asset. He consistently achieved his targets, with yearly sales always surpassing every goal. His eye was on the sky, and nothing could stop him.

Carl not only poured his heart into his work, but he went above and beyond for everyone. He truly cared for the people he engaged with, and that kindness was apparent with every interaction. Aware of the world's challenges, he often provided cautionary advice to those he perceived as vulnerable. "Be careful out here because smiling faces aren't always your friends." He was always sure to point that out. "Hope, there will come a day when

I won't be around anymore. People will show their hands and you need to be wise. Promise me, you'll never forget that I truly loved you."

In those moments, I was confused. It was like a mysterious riddle. What was he talking about? How could he have known or felt what would later be one of the hardest moments in my lifetime? One event that would change me as a person, as a spiritual soul in need of deliverance, as a woman with direction and purpose who would face ridicule and scrutiny and come face to face with her greatest challenge. Who could have known the horrific events that would unfold?

I was left with questions more than answers and Carl never explained what he meant. Life seemed to move along somehow suspended in time. The hardest moments that took me back to a place where my fears and my faith waged war against my soul.

Chapter Two

The shrill ringing of the phone abruptly awaken me, shattering the silence of the early morning. I reached for Carl, but his side of the bed was cold. In my half-awake daze, I remembered he was stopping by his mother's house after work.

As I fumbled to answer the phone, the voice on the other end sounded weak and distressed. I recognized the voice as Carl's sister, Gina. She sounded distant, like she could barely speak as she searched for the words to explain the reason for her call.

"Hope, Carl is dead. He's been shot. His body was found beside the roadway inside of his car." She broke off briefly, sobbing. "Hang on, there is someone here who would like to speak with you. Hold on for me."

I heard the words she spoke, but I couldn't find my voice to speak. It was as if someone ripped out my voice box and shoved a baseball into my throat. As I attempted to swallow, my throat tightened. My heart wrenched from its rhythm, and I suddenly lost the air in my lungs to breathe.

"Ma'am? I am so sorry for your loss, but I would like to speak with you in person as soon as possible." Who was the voice?

"No, no, please. It can't be true! This is not real." I wanted to scream, but I couldn't. I wanted to run until my chest no longer burned with fire, but I couldn't.

"I am very sorry ma'am, but it is true." The voice spoke again. I just wanted to die at that very moment.

Every effort to speak felt restricted and cut off. I opened my mouth to say something, anything, but I was in shock. I just sat there on the edge of the bed holding the phone in disbelief. How could this have happened? I just spoke to Carl earlier that evening and now he was gone.

Our dreams of a wedding in Texas and our life together now lay in ruins. It felt as though my life was unfolding, like the scenes from a movie slowly playing out before me.

Thoughts raced through my mind, yet I struggled to grasp their meaning. Tears flowed uncontrollably down my cheeks, overflowing from my eyes. Just the thought of telling my son, Bentley, made me cringe. How could I find the words to tell him such devastating news?

The pain was indescribable; it surpassed all other losses in my life. I had already lost two brothers and my father; how could I go on without Carl? He was more than just a partner; he was my best friend. Who could have done this to him?

I felt my body slowly sliding to the floor. I was still holding the phone with the voice still on the other end of the line. "Ma'am? Ma'am, are you there?"

My feet felt as if they were encased in cement and my heart thudded painfully against my ribcage. I felt paralyzed. The world was spinning around me in a surreal haze. I closed my eyes as I fought to catch my breath and answer the voice.

"Yes. I'm here."

The voice identified himself as Detective Albert Thomas ABI, the officer investigating the case and the one who reported the incident to Carl's family. His voice was crisp and authoritative, a weapon within itself as it delivered the devastating news. It was followed by a heavy silence, broken only by Gina's return.

"Carl had multiple gunshot wounds to his body. The authorities haven't told us much at this point."

That was all she could say. Her words landed heavily in the pit of my stomach like anvils. Each word weighed on my heart as she spoke them with a hollow voice. Shock held me in its icy grip while my world shattered into tiny pieces. Why Carl? What about his children? And...Janet.

For the past fourteen months, Carl had taken up residence in his childhood home, living with his mother, Mary, while he waited for his painfully slow and complex divorce to reach its long-awaited conclusion.

Carl and Janet tried for a long time to reconcile, but there was no hope and she merely held on to make his life hell. She pretended to be an abused wife, and she didn't hide her infidelity either.

Janet was a wildflower, untamable and free, dancing in the wind and gathering admirers like petals in her hair. She would flirt and dance with her suitors, never staying with just one for very long.

Despite her seedy nightlife, Janet was known for her warm smile and kind demeanor, but there were moments when her facade would slip. Carl noticed it during their late-night conversations, catching a fleeting glimpse of her coldness. Her behavior usually led to arguments and Carl watching Janet storm out of the house. Soon he grew tired of trying to save a marriage that was already lost, and he was the only one fighting for it. They parted ways but the divorce seemed to linger on and on. As if time slowed to an infinite stop.

Time? Now seemed to stand perfectly still. I could hear each tick, tick, tick, tick of the clock as it echoed through the lonely room. Each second felt like an eternity as the walls felt like a cage. The sound was suffocating me as time dragged on at a painfully slow pace.

My heart raced wildly while I tried to process these moments and tame my emotions. I slowly gathered the willpower to call my mom and close friends. I asked my brother, Keithan, and his wife Natalie to accompany me to Mary's house to be with the family.

My mind was a jumbled mess, too foggy to focus on anything, as I stumbled towards the chest of drawers in search of suitable clothing. With shaking hands, I fumbled with buttons and zippers until I was finally dressed. I heard a knock at the door and knew it was Keithan.

"I am sorry sis! Dammit, this hurts." His expression was tense and rigid. There was nothing I could say as we climbed into his truck and left the apartment.

Mary's ranch style two-story home with blue chipping paint gave me a foreboding feeling. The once inviting and familiar place was now a stark contrast to my inner turmoil. Like a silent sentinel, Mary stood on the front porch, her eyes red and puffy from crying.

The air inside the living room was heavy with sadness. Each person was draped in their own shroud of anger and disbelief.

Carl's death crushed the spirits of all those close to him. He was such a gentle soul. So heartfelt and personable, undeserving of such savage acts. To be gunned down like an animal and left on the highway for someone to find was unimaginable. We all wanted answers and to find those responsible. I would do anything to get justice for his murder.

As I watched the faces of Carl's family, I could only think of how much they were hurting. Some spoke about getting justice in any way they could. Others speculated on their suspicions in small group huddles. They were all devastated. It was just too much to deal with.

Feeling numb from the shock, my legs teetered on the brink of weakness. A chill coursed through my veins as I stared blankly, fixed on the white wall in front of me. The room seemed to spin as I struggled to process the reality of Carl's absence. It was like I was still waiting for him to walk through the door. I desperately wanted to hear him say how it was all just a big mistake. But even as I clung to this hope, I knew he wouldn't be coming back.

All the pressure I had built up in my chest felt like a million shards of shattered glass, slowly slicing away at my soul until nothing remained.

"Baby, you be careful! You stay with your family and don't be alone at any time. The dogs that took my son may try to take you!" Mary turned to me and took my hands in hers. "My son loved you with all his heart and I know this because he told me so. I've never seen him so happy before in all his days. Know that we love you. Don't you ever forget that!"

Tears rolled from her eyes and down her face, filling her lids so full and heavy. Her heart was broken. Her child was taken from her, gone forever. My chest felt tight as my heart cried out with hers. I just wanted to make it stop.

To see her suffering was like watching life drain from her very existence and deplete from her being. It was sheer agony. Her shoulders shook with deep, guttural sobs as she gazed at the empty space where her son used to sit in his favorite chair. Each exhale was a struggle, as if an invisible hand was squeezing the air from her lungs. Her cheeks burned hot as tears smeared the carefully applied mascara into dark rivers. I looked on until I just couldn't stand it any longer.

We lingered for a bit until Keithan inquired about my readiness to head home and rest. I sighed and glanced up at him in silence. Keithan's voice sounded distant when he asked, and rest was just unthinkable. How could I possibly rest? I felt like I was standing on the edge of a bottomless abyss. I feared taking one wrong step and disappearing forever. Although I knew that I'd have to take that step eventually, I first had to catch my breath.

As I looked around the room at Carl's family, I felt pieces of me dying off. I needed air. I took a deep breath and motioned my hand as if to say I was leaving.

"Are you about to go? You need to get on home and stay there, be safe." Gina looked at me as if she knew my vacuity. I nodded and embraced her, then Mary, as Keithan glanced over and acknowledged my readiness for departure. I understood why he wanted to go. He was just as stunned by the events as we all were and just concerned for my safety. Everyone felt the need to be on guard, wondering what else could happen and who the next victim might be.

Natalie had remained hushed throughout, yet she was comforting and supportive. She offered comforting words and gentle gestures with her soft voice. Her shy posture gave her a delicate appearance, accented by streaks of grey in her long brown hair. Despite standing at an impressive height, she seemed almost ethereal with her pale complexion and conservative clothing that portrayed her humble spirit.

I couldn't help but admire Natalie for her patience and understanding towards my brother. She put up with his waywardness and all his complexities for years. Keithan was a hell-raiser now and again but could also be a giving, polite person, ready to help everyone. I'd seen him give his last to the needy, but he was also an addict.

Despite his demons, he held down a steady job and had periods of sobriety. But drugs and alcohol were constantly tugging at him, threatening to take away his future. We all feared that one day, addiction would claim him like it had taken so many others we knew. Natalie tried to help, but Keithan always found his way back.

Keithan was a hard shell of relentless demands and unquenchable needs. It was exhausting, yet Natalie was unwavering in her determination to make things work between them. Her patience and dedication remained steadfast throughout the worst of times.

"Let's get you on home now." Natalie took my hand as we made our way to Keithan's truck. As we drove away, we could feel the neighbors' eyes on us, as if we were misplaced, lost and uncertain. It was a feeling like everyone on the planet had vanished and we were the only survivors left.

Still and quiet with nothing moving but the truck, the motor hummed along the empty road. The ride was indifferent, lonely, and vacated in feeling. No one spoke as if we didn't quite know how to communicate, almost like strangers. Finally, Keithan spoke up.

"You shouldn't stay by yourself right now. I am taking you to mamas." I could hear the worry in his voice. But I was beyond caring about my destination; all I wanted to do was disappear.

My mind was in a terrible place because my heart was bleeding. I was still looking for Carl, searching the day like he would pop up in the tapestry of time. Where was he? My eyes fell upon every car we passed on the highway, hoping to catch a glimpse of him. My heart was still in denial, and I knew I had to let go of the hope. Blinking back tears and biting my lip until it drew blood, I struggled to hold onto my emotions.

As we drove along the highway, the trees formed a corridor on either side of the road. Their leaves rustling in the wind, dancing with fluidity and grace. Through the side window, the glow of the city lights painted a vibrant orange and yellow against the deep blue of the horizon.

I could picture my mom with her hands clenched tightly in front of her. The wrinkles in her forehead deepening as she waited for us to arrive. I knew she'd be there with Bentley standing close by her side.

The thought of returning home filled me with a sense of comfort and warmth that I longed for. A familiar warmth and contentment that beckoned me back to where I belonged.

The embrace of my mom and Bentley made my world stand still in a moment of tenderness, like a cocoon of solace. It provided a temporary escape from the harsh, painful reality. A soothing balm for my mind. But it was the night that proved to be most challenging and unforgiving. Insomnia settled in, tightening its grip with each passing moment. Somewhere in the bewitching hours, I drifted off into a deep sleep.

The morning came quickly as I awoke with a jolt, blinking in the early morning light as it poured through the window and danced across the laminate wood flooring beneath me. The soft sheets were twisted around my body and memories of Carl came flooding back to me. His voice, our adventures together, the smell of his cologne; all of it coming back in vivid detail.

I rested for a while, transfixed by a notion of ambivalence that seemed to fill the room. It was as if time was suspended, and all just a dream. I surveyed every detail of the half-open drawers of mom's antique chest, trying to organize my rambling thoughts.

The room was filled with familiar scents and sounds, but they all seemed fuddled and unreal to me. I closed my eyes and breathed deeply, trying to hold onto a sense of reality. The sounds, smells, and voices blurred together into an indistinguishable haze. Then a heaviness settled over me, and just for a moment nothing mattered.

Mom entered the room, and it was the look on her face that confirmed my worst fears. I wanted to die. Just vanish. Her eyes filled with tears as she sat down beside me, placing a gentle hand on my shoulder. I laid my head on her chest and sobbed. It felt like all my emotions had been drained, leaving only an overwhelming sense of pain. But like a current of electricity, it hit me, I remembered that I had an appointment.

"You should eat something, Hope." Mom hugged me tightly.

"I can't."

I shifted my gaze to the digital clock on the nightstand. Time seemed to be moving too quickly as I dreaded getting out of bed and facing the day ahead. But I knew I couldn't miss my appointment with ABI. They may have new information about Carl's death, details that were purposely left out by the media. Each answer could hold vital clues in tracking down his killer, and justice was all I wanted for him, more than anything else.

"You can't pour from an empty cup," Mom insisted, her voice tense with worry. I couldn't bring myself to eat, not with everything that had happened.

"Maybe later, Mom," I said, trying to keep my voice steady. "I think I'll just take a shower first." She nodded, understanding my need for some time alone.

After savoring the lingering warmth of my shower, I quickly dressed and made my way to Bentley. He was bright eyed and awaiting me in the living room. We embraced tightly, then I grabbed my purse and stepped out into the crisp morning air. A slight mist covered the ground as I drove away, the headlights of my car illuminating the winding road that led me to Montgomery.

Upon my arrival at headquarters, I was greeted and escorted into a small drab conference room where two detectives were present. We sat down at a gray metal table that gleamed like a sheet of polished steel, its sharp edges cutting through the dullness of the room. The four chairs stood at attention, their metal frames waiting to be filled, creating an atmosphere of stoic readiness.

Two detectives proceeded to ask many questions about my relationship with Carl, his relationship with others, his driving habits, and then one explained what happened to him in horrid detail.

"Ma'am, I am very sorry, but what I am about to say may be quite difficult for you to hear." He slid a brightly colored box of Kleenex across the table until the box rested within my hands' reach. Shaking profusely, I reached for a tissue.

"From what we have gathered, Carl was seen arguing with someone the night of his murder. They apparently followed him, and later ambushed him on the highway." The detective stopped and stared at me as if waiting for my reaction. He then went on to say that Carl was already dead when they arrived on the scene.

While the detective was giving the graven details of the incident, I still couldn't believe that I lived that day as my reality. I wanted to wake up from my emotional wreck and see Carl walking through the door. I glanced over at the doorway several times seeking his face, awaiting his entrance to the room, all smiles.

My eyes kept searching for any sign of him, his face peering through the small square glass in the conference room door. For a second, I could almost see him there. I could hear his voice saying to me, "I truly love you! I will always love you!" His face glistening and beaming but fading as my eyes became full and blurred. I blinked to readjust my vision, but he wasn't there. He never came. Where was he? Didn't he know how much I needed to see him? Just to hear his voice one more time.

I felt desolate and dazed. My chest was an inferno burning so hot as if it were on fire. My neck was bathed in tears. I couldn't stop them from falling from my eyes, drenching my face, and rolling under my chin. As I wiped them away, I felt how raw and inflamed my sockets were. My breaths became shallow and my palms sweaty. A wave of nausea washed over me with a daunting notion, "I can't do this!" Silently pleading, "God, make it stop, I cannot handle this!" But did He hear me? Was He listening?

Sitting there, as the investigator divulged the horrific details of the incident, I felt like I was in a different realm of sorts. Like I was somewhere else and living somebody else's life. In a room that was cold and sterile, the walls painted a dull shade of grey. The only source of light was a flickering fluorescent bulb in the corner, casting an eerie glow on the detective's face. His features were sharp and angular, his eyes hidden behind a pair of thin-framed glasses. He looked at me with a mixture of pity and curiosity as he finished his report.

"Would you like a few minutes, ma'am?"

Unknowing if I nodded or said anything at all, the detectives stepped away and left me sitting there alone. Through a passthrough window, I could see them in an adjoining room. Lots of nods and hand motions were exchanged between them. What a mess they must have thought about me: a bucket or a basket case, maybe both. I could see them peering at me in observance of my emotions and body language. Reading me and noting my confusion.

Shifting my weight on the hard, uncomfortable chair, my mind replayed the last time I saw Carl. How his clothes hugged his chiseled muscular physique. How bright and infectious his smile was as we said our good-byes. I recalled the dreamy look in his eyes when he told me that he loved me and how much I now longed for those little things. I remembered the nights before the shooting when Carl said his feet hurt and how he thought it was a sign of something ominous.

My mind was filled with every detail; the sound of his laugh, the way he would fidget with his keys when nervous, and the warmth of his hand on mine. But amidst all the happy moments were the haunting ones. Those that stuck with me and refused to grant me peace. The ones I begged God to put behind me.

Moments afterward, the two detectives came back into the room. "Ma'am, that is all we have for now. Stay safe and always be aware of your surroundings. Keep in contact with us. It's very important." I nodded my head as I rose from my chair.

"Thank you both for your continued efforts to investigate Carl's murder. I pray you find those responsible for this."

I stumbled out of the interrogation room, my stomach growling loudly from the lack of food. My eyes were heavy with exhaustion and barely staying open. Despite my weariness, I knew I had to make the long drive back home – sixty miles down the lonely highway. I had to stay awake and alert.

Closing the car door, I just sat there gripping the steering wheel tightly. The traumatic memories flooded my mind as I drifted off into a daze. Remembering the sound of my doorbell ringing and ringing, the gunshots that still echoed in my ears. I could feel the intense fear and adrenaline coursing through me once again.

Someone tried to take my life just last week and it was still fresh in my mind, replaying over and over horridly and I couldn't escape. I drifted back into those moments trying to relive the events as if to piece it all together.

I became lost in the memories of that traumatic night.

Chapter Three

C arl was working out of town when it happened. Bentley was sleeping upstairs across the hall from my room and had been down about an hour. It was a typical Wednesday night, quiet and uneventful. The digital clock on my nightstand displayed 11:30 p.m. I was curled up in bed watching late night television.

The sudden ringing of the doorbell startled me as it seemed odd to have a visitor at that hour. I paused, doubting myself for a moment, like maybe I didn't hear it. But then, there it was again - *Ding Dong* - no mistake this time. The consistent ringing of the bell was alarming. I crept towards the window, peering through the glass to catch a glimpse of anyone lurking outside my door. The moonless night made it difficult to see. I blamed myself for not turning on the porch light before retiring for the evening.

The night was deep and dark; the stars hidden by the thick blanket of clouds. The nearby area was shrouded in blackness, with no streetlamp to provide any semblance of light.

The bell rang incessantly, breaking the eerie silence. I hesitated, unsure if I should answer the door. What if it's something important? And if it's family they'd call first. Or would they? With cautious steps, I descended the stairs.

The doorbell's insistent chimes echoed throughout the house, signaling that the visitor was not giving up easily. I stopped at the bottom of the stairs and hesitated for a moment. Step by step, I made my way towards the front door, but instead of looking through the peephole I simply leaned in closer to listen. I knew it was too dark outside to see, so I just stood there, trying to figure out what to do.

There I was, home alone, with a small child. What should I do? Perhaps ignore it. I remained still and listened but there was no movement. Listening for a voice or a noise through the door or any sound from the other side, I put my ear to the crack in the door, leaning in with my left side. Carl had placed a recliner adjacent to the front of the door, so I positioned my body precisely as I pushed against the door frame.

With just the tip of my shoulder touching the line in between, I spoke, "Who is it?" I didn't get a reply from anyone on the other side. I just stood there leaning in, motionless. *Bang, bang, bang, bang, bang, bang*, six shots rang out! Terrified, I wasn't sure what to do. It happened so fast! I felt my body moving but I wasn't going anywhere, as if I were running in place. Panic set in.

I heard the sharp crack of ceramics. The plant pedestal hit the floor off to my right. Shards flew in every direction, some landing on the carpet and some skittering across the tile. My body trembled and shook. I wondered if I should dive for the couch or fall to the floor. Be still or wait?

Shaking uncontrollably, I broke and ran into the bathroom thinking, "Oh my God, I'm going to get hit!" Once inside, I fell to the floor. "Oh God, please help me!" I frantically whispered, words barely coming out of my mouth; muffled, and panicked. Am I hit? Am I bleeding? I felt around for wounds or anything wet. All I could do was kneel on the floor and plead for His protection. I was disoriented and rattled in a moment of terror and harrowing fear.

Still patting myself down, the sounds around me seemed deafened. Was I in pain? I kept feeling and checking my body. I looked in the mirror to see any visible signs of injury. Oh! The shooter! Are they gone? Then immediately I thought about Bentley. I had to get to him! He was sleeping upstairs at the top of the staircase. All those bullets! Oh my God, the bullets! Did they get Bentley?

I heard a car outside speeding away quickly, tires squealing on the pavement. At that point I came out of the bathroom and rushed to get Bentley.

Ignoring the shards of glass and debris scattered across the tiled floor, I sprinted barefoot towards the stairwell. My heart raced as my mind spiraled with panicked thoughts, all focused on one thing: reaching my baby. I looked up at the stairs and saw bullet holes riddling the walls, sending a surge of terror through me. My feet pounded against the wood steps as I desperately tried to reach Bentley's room.

As I ascended the stairs, my heart beating against my chest, not knowing what I would see when I reached Bentley's room. The bullet holes in the wall at the top of the staircase confirmed my fears and sent me into a panic. I burst into his room and ran to his bedside, my hands trembling as I checked for any sign of life.

Bentley lay there, his small frame still and peaceful, but there was a faint rise and fall of his chest that gave me hope. "Please God," I whispered as tears streamed down my face. Was he breathing? I yanked the covers back to examine him closely. I placed my hand on his chest, feeling for a heartbeat and any sign of life. In that instant, I knew God heard me. He saw me and He heard me. How could Bentley have slept through all that noise?

Amazingly, he was still resting soundly and never heard a single shot. He was untouched. Only Jah could have protected my child. If ever I knew Jehovah loved us, I knew it at that moment. He saw me, and He heard me. He saved us.

I dropped to my knees, overcome with emotion. The world seemed to stop as my heart raced against my breath. It was like I had been hit in the chest, and all the air knocked out of my lungs. With each gasping wheeze, my legs became unsteady, turning to shaky Jell-O beneath me.

My hands trembled uncontrollably as I lay helplessly on the floor, unable to summon any strength to move towards the distant phone. My body felt frail and weak in a moment of desperation.

I rose to my feet and staggered my way to the bedroom. My fingers fumbled for the phone. The handset glimmered in the faint lighting, its screen dark and unresponsive. My vision blurred and I couldn't make out the numbers. I kept blinking rapidly, struggling to bring the keypad into focus. Carefully dialing each number until an operator came on the line.

"911, what's your emergency?"

Though my mouth moved no sound would escape. I attempted to explain the situation, but it was no use. Each time I tried to speak I could only gasp for air. The operator asked, "Hello? Is anyone there?" I kept trying to form coherent words, but all that came out was gibberish. Panic was making it hard to think.

"Ma'am, calm down. Tell me what happened." Gibberish again. "Ma'am, slow down; breathe."

Finally, I gathered enough air into my lungs and asked for help. "Someone shot up my apartment! I need help." My throat felt constricted.

"Are you hurt? Is anyone there with you?" The operator's voice was firm but soothing.

"No." The crack of the gunshots still rang in my ears, punctuating every thought.

"Ok, ma'am, help is on the way. I will stay on the line with you until they arrive."

I was still trying to breathe. Why couldn't I breathe? Someone just tried to take my life! The realization sent a paralyzing chill down my spine and my legs threatened to give way beneath me. Oh my God, why?

Questions flooded my mind. I was so confused. Bentley and I could have died! We always kept to ourselves and were well-respected in our community. This was just unthinkable. Maybe they made a mistake and thought this was someone else's apartment. That could happen.

My head was spinning, and I struggled to stay conscious by taking deep breaths and trying to steady myself. I took one step forward and then another until I reached the wall, where I leaned against it for support.

Bentley was still sleeping, and the less he knew the better. With bated breath, I entered the stairway, cautiously descending each step downward. As I reached the bottom, my heart pounded against my ribcage. My eyes fixated on the shattered pieces of glass scattered about and a litter of plaster from the whatnots no longer recognizable. I knew we were blessed to be alive. I put my head in my hands and sat in disbelief.

Knock, Knock, Knock.

I gasped. They're back! I could feel my pulse pounding. My gaze flickered to the door, my heart racing with anticipation. My mouth went dry, and my tongue felt like sandpaper as I tried to swallow the lump in my throat. My body stiffened. I felt the hairs on the back of my neck stand up as goosebumps erupted across my skin.

"The officers' have arrived."

Still not convinced, I stared at the door for several minutes.

"Ma'am, did you hear me?" The operator asked.

"Selma Police Dept!"

I was afraid to open the door. Even after I heard the officers identify themselves. if it wasn't the police?

I warily approached the doorway with the phone still in my hand. Reaching for the door with one hand, shaking, turning the knob inch by inch until I could see the door opening getting wider and wider. Peering cautiously around the other side, sweat beading across my brow. There they were. Standing in the doorway were two police officers.

"Ma'am? Are you okay?" One officer asked, looking at me with wide eyes of circumspect.

"Yes, I think so." I exhaled the breath I was holding and thanked the operator on the phone for staying with me.

After letting the officers inside, they assessed the damages and processed the scene while making out their report. They spoke with neighbors who, surprisingly, said they did not hear any gunfire.

Both officers asked if I knew of anyone who might want to harm me. Now that was the real question! I couldn't imagine anyone being my enemy and wanting to kill me. But then my mind had an interesting thought. No, it couldn't be. Or could it?

I took a seat on the couch and surveyed the chaos before me. My front door, once a symbol of security, was riddled with bullet holes. A sense of dread settled in, adding to the tension already building in the room. The voice inside my head grew louder as I gave way to sobs, while the ticking of the clock punctuated every passing second.

It was a long night and although it seemed endless, gratitude swept over me. I was so thankful that Bentley didn't wake up during the shooting and thankful that my baby was not hurt or disturbed. I was so rattled and frightened, but comforted by the simple fact that we were alive. God was looking out for us. Who was I to deserve His loving kindness? He shielded me and my son, and there was no doubt in my mind about that. I reflected on the book of Psalms, *"He rescued me from my strong enemy."* Whomever the enemy may be, they are not stronger than God Almighty.

As the officers examined the scene, they noticed multiple bullet holes in the door. One of them pointed out that if I had been standing and looking through the peephole, the bullets would have struck me directly in the chest. It was a chilling realization that the shooter must have known my height and positioning to make such an accurate and deadly shot. But why?

My front door resembled a crime scene from a prime-time TV series. The holes were strategically placed next to each other in the door with precision, forming a haunting narrative. All I could do was stare at them, absorbing the silent testimony of the harrowing experience. I looked on as if I were observing someone else's house and certainly not the place I called home. I kept toiling over it, searching for answers. Who could hate me so much? All I had were questions.

My thoughts never stopped playing out the event over and over again. I was searching for answers that I did not have. Trying to assemble a puzzle without all the pieces was challenging. One big jigsaw. I was trying to convince myself that surely it was random, or maybe a case of mistaken identity. I recalled the police leaving my apartment just as Carl arrived home. It was shortly after that Bentley appeared and saw the chaos in the living room.

"What happened here, ma?"

As I looked at his innocent little face, I tried to choose my words carefully when I spoke to him. It was so disheartening to tell my nine-year-old child that our home was dismantled by gunfire while he slept. I couldn't bring myself to admit or even acknowledge the obvious. I also could not lie to him. Bentley was so intelligent and too smart not to figure it out.

Choosing my words gently to explain, the look on his face was heart wrenching. I could see the fear creeping up into his eyes, intensifying. I just held Bentley close and tried to give him some sort of comfort. I kept assuring him that everything was going to be okay. We were going to be fine. Carl, however, was livid and just kept pacing the floor.

"Who would commit such a low and cowardly act? You can't stay here. We will do what we can for this door, but you must leave here tonight!" He insisted as he examined the damage. We gathered our belongings and got ready to depart.

Anxiety crept in as I thought about potential dangers awaiting us. Peering through the back door, Carl cautiously stepped out, scanning the area. Following closely behind him, I heard rustling in the nearby bushes. My heart skipped a beat, and I froze in fear. Carl saw me and immediately said, "Get back in the house!" I pushed Bentley behind me to shelter him and quickly shut the door behind us. Then the door swung open. I leaned backward to brace myself for whatever was on the other side.

"It's ok. It was just a cat," said Carl. My heart sank with relief.

"You scared me!" I let out a deep breath. With a relieved look, Carl smiled.

"I'm sorry. Let's get out of here."

Inside the car, Bentley wore a curious expression. "Where are we going ma?" With a slight smile, I reassured him. "To stay with granny for a while." He appeared content with the response. Bentley always looked forward to seeing his granny, and it was important to me that he felt comfortable and secure. I couldn't think of a better place for us to be than with her.

All too eager to leave the apartment as quickly as possible, I glanced around anxiously as we drove away. Carl followed closely behind us to make sure we made our destination safely. We stayed with my mom for a week before returning to the apartment to get any of our things, and we could not go there alone.

The feeling of home had been shattered, leaving me unsettled in my own space. I felt I had been violated, robbed, assaulted, or just stripped down to bare bones. The place we once called home now felt like a trap, stuck in a perpetual loop, endlessly reliving that terrifying night. I knew it would never be our home again. Carl seemed to be convinced that the goons would not come back and try again, but why did they ever try at all? What was the motive?

I developed a phobia from that experience and before stepping outside, I would always glance out the window first. No matter which door I approached, I was in fear all the time. Constantly looking over my shoulders and jumping at every unexpected noise. Our once carefree lives had become consumed by fear and uncertainty.

Carl and I huddled together, trying to figure out who could be after me. He was so focused on protecting me that we couldn't even imagine the danger that awaited us. If only we had known the truth, perhaps we could have prepared ourselves for what was yet to come. Possibly even saved his life.

Now shifting my focus back to the present and coming out of my daze, I was still sitting in my car outside ABI headquarters. Recalling my near-death experience only brought me more grief. Inhaling a deep breath, I pushed the key into the ignition and started the car.

Backing out of the parking lot, my mind was replaying the traumatic details of Carl's murder. The ABI interrogation about Carl's life and activities only added to the strange and hollow feelings inside me. My fiancé had been ripped away from me in the blink of an eye. I was absolutely destroyed.

A profound sense of isolation enveloped me. I'd never encountered such a poignant experience. Losing someone abruptly is one thing but losing them in such a tragic manner adds another layer of anguish. Carl was savagely taken from a loving family that cherished him deeply. A life gone that could never be replaced.

The road stretched out like a ribbon of memories, each mile a marker of the tumultuous events that had unfolded in such a short time. It called to mind those cinematic moments where someone is sitting behind an old film reel, looking back in time, and dissecting their past. The memories, the laughs, and the faces. I couldn't stop seeing Carl's expression. The look he had when he said he felt something. Like the burning sensation in his feet that was unfamiliar, leaving him bewildered by its significance. I thought maybe he was ill, but he said, "No, I don't know, something is brewing and, well, I may be next." Next for what?

On the drive home, I kept telling myself that I had to prepare for things to come. I had to think of more than just myself and I wasn't the only one hurting. This was going to be a journey that Bentley and I could not walk alone. Now more than ever, we relied on each other and needed a solid support system. We had to watch our backs.

For our families and closest friends, the news was staggering, and yet its reality was hard to accept. We all had to find our own way through this unfathomable loss. We had to learn how to navigate each day going forward. Most of all Mary. She needed to discover how to heal from her loss, her heart now battered, entirely composed of sorrow, and her spirit broken.

Her face from our last visit remained etched in my memory, a stark contrast to the woman I once adored before Carl's passing. I thought about how her face exuded so much pain. The loss was draining Mary of her glowing light, a golden aura that she carried with grace. A light that complemented her warm and glowing smile.

Now in her sixties, her shoulders drooped with age, but she never tired of energy or the joy of cruising around town in her beautiful Jaguar that Carl bought for her. He'd saved for years to buy his beloved mother the car of her dreams and gifted it to her shortly before his passing. She was so proud of Carl. He was her cornerstone.

Mary most graciously welcomed Bentley and me into her family. The Fishers showed us so much concern and consideration. They were supportive of Carl and I building a successful life together and we had it all it seemed. But someone out there did not want that for us. Someone out there was determined to destroy our lives at any cost and that someone was ruthless, cunning, wicked, and relentless. I couldn't brush off the fear that they would strike again. My mind swirling with thoughts of when and how. It was hard to fathom that they were finished with us since I was still alive. Alive, but dead inside. A shell of a person trying to exist; hollow and empty, going through the motions of life.

But then my thoughts shifted, fixating on Bentley and how fiercely determined I was to protect him at any cost. I had to be strong for him, even if it meant using every ounce of my strength and blood. That was all that mattered to me. I would do anything for him. Bentley was my anchor and while my thoughts were consumed by so many things, he was always my main concern.

I took in a deep breath and blinked my eyes as the sun light filtered through the tree line. The flickering and dancing of light across my vision brought my attention back from the past and onto the road ahead. Like a thousand tiny kaleidoscopes, the flickering made me dizzy as I made the final turn towards home.

By now, Bentley must have been anxious about my well-being, and I felt the need to call my mother to check in. My hand instinctively reached for the car phone, but I was reminded that Carl never installed a new one. We just never got around to it. The memory of the shattered phone lying on the asphalt after my near crippling car wreck flashed before me. Although a year later, I was still healing from another difficult experience that had caused me great pain.

I pushed my car a little harder down the highway to get home quickly. I was terrified by every vehicle that passed or lingered behind me. I remained in a constant qualm, feeling watched and tracked like an animal. Just never knowing. Dry fear coated my tongue, making it difficult to swallow as I imagined the worst scenarios in my head. While fear may have been behind the wheel, I knew that God's eyes were on his sparrow.

As I arrived home Bentley ran out to greet me. Always full of smiles and happiness, such a beautiful child. His luxurious soft brown curls and big, bright brown eyes complimented his sweet little face. I hugged him tightly, not wanting to let him go. His vibrant smile brought light to my face and lifted me up above the clouds. Here was a child so carefree and full of life. Jehovah's blessing indeed.

We were joined at the hip, my Bentley and me. I gave him a little kiss on his cheek as we walked inside where mom was standing at the side door entrance.

"How did your appointment go?" Mom put her arm around me and gave me a gentle squeeze.

"It was fine, mom. I'm just glad it's over." I gave her a nod and a smile.

"Come on inside and have some coffee with me." Relieved that I made the trip safely, she wasn't one to ask twenty questions.

"Go sit at the table and eat something," Mom encouraged, placing a plate filled with a delicious meal in front of me. But I couldn't muster up any hunger. Ever since Carl's passing, my appetite had disappeared, and food no longer held any appeal to me. "You are going to wither away if you don't eat."

With Bentley watching me as if to witness my first bite of food, I pretended to take a bite of scalloped potatoes. His smile warmed me through and through as my eyes filled with tears that I fought to withhold.

"Good job, mom. You have to grow big and strong like me." Bentley said so lovingly.

Once Bentley left the table, Mom questioned my attendance at Carl's services, expressing worry and advising against it.

"Hope, I am not so sure it's a good idea for us to attend these services."

"Mom, it's ok. We will have lots of friends and family with us."

"You've been through enough, don't you think? People will stare at you in that church. Doesn't that bother you?" She had that troubled look on her face, and I knew what that meant.

"Mom, we have to pay our respects to Carl."

"Sweetie, we all loved him. My concern now is for your safety." Mom didn't seem to be fully sold on my suggestion.

"Mom, please. I have to do this. For Carl." Touching mom's hand, I gave her a gentle smile.

"Okay. But I am not letting you go alone." Mom furrowed her brows, the lines between them deepening as she spoke steadily and firmly. I slowly nodded my head in agreement and brought the steaming white mug of coffee to my lips. The warm vapor tickled my nose while I lifted my chin ever so slightly and took a sip.

"I need to find something to wear." Mom rose from the table, her movements deliberate and heavy. I could hear her humming as she began searching through her closet.

Mom's words about clothing jolted a realization: Bentley and I needed outfits. I hadn't considered our attire until now, so I immediately checked our closets for options. With limited funds, a shopping trip was not one of them. Instead, I retrieved some of my favorite pieces from the back of the closet and tried them on. Relieved that I could easily mix and match pieces that I already had, I laid out a black jacket with white trim, a black pencil skirt, and black heels that coordinated perfectly.

Bentley had a selection of three cute ties, a couple of dress slacks, and two suit jackets to choose from for the funeral. He chose his favorite black pinstriped slacks that were slightly wrinkled and matched them to the black pinstriped suit jacket and black dress shoes.

"Where is your shirt, Bentley?"

"I like the white one with the creases, mom." He smiled and pointed to the closet. I reached inside to grab his chosen item.

"You have great taste." I complimented him as we completed our ensemble and set everything aside.

The thought of attending this memorial was like a rusted knife blade against my skin, a constant ache that refused to dull. I debated if I should take Bentley along. I wondered if he would want to stay behind but I was also too afraid to leave him. What were we going to do with this life of ours now? We were too afraid to go and too afraid to stay.

Chapter Four

I n the days leading up to the service, we had a host of visitors come to the house. Some brought food and condolences, while others brought rumors and questions. Others arrived to assess our company and identify the ones holding everything together.

In the corners, under dim lighting, whispers could be heard seeping from their lips as their eyes scanned the room. Others sat on the porch and talked among themselves, choosing not to set one foot inside the house to console the family.

Inside or out, a noticeable air of uneasiness assumed company among those gathered; almost uncomfortable. It was awkward. Some neighbors dropped off bags of groceries and sympathy cards, while others gave hugs and sat with my mom making small talk.

Keithan and Natalie were unpacking food items and setting plates; serving those interested in a meal and hospitality. Natalie moved about the kitchen like a hummingbird in a garden of possibility. As she worked, she hummed an old tune, one that her father had sung to her when she was a child. Its notes were soothing, and guests stood watching in awe the way she arranged everything with such precision and care. Keithan was her helper and took instructions as Natalie gave them.

The house was abuzz with conversation, the walls barely containing the voices of a dozen friends and family members spilling out of the kitchen. Some of them had known each other for years, their conversations filled with laughter and teasing. Others were strangers, connected only through the shared tragedy that had brought them all together.

I felt the day waning on me, so I quietly retreated to my room where I often nested, avoiding people. I just wasn't feeling their energy, nor did I have any of my own to give. I needed to find some consolation, if that was even possible but I knew it would not come from pretending to entertain the various conversations among our guests.

For the most part, my escape plan was proving successful. Occasionally, someone would impose on my solitude with that overly concerned expression. Their long stares and wandering gazes revealed their struggle to communicate with me, but we all understood the intent. Despite this, everyone did their best to offer sympathies in their own way, and that was enough for me.

There was, however, one guest I never anticipated seeing and she was standing in my doorway.

"Hope, if you have a minute, I have something to say to you." Janet stood before me, her eyes tense with emotion. Her black dress was form fitting to her small athletic frame.

"Sure. Have a seat." Startled, I motioned to the wicker chair in the corner.

"I know we have our differences, but we grieve for the same man. We both loved him, and everything is just so raw right now. I just want you to know that I am here if you want to talk about this."

I stared at Janet, not sure of what to say. Clearing my throat, I made an honest gesture.

"Janet, I know this must be uncomfortable for you, coming here. I am actually very surprised to see you. However, I appreciate your extension of kindness. That really means a lot." A brief silence filled the air.

"Understood. I was worried you might not want to see me." She reached inside her purse, fidgeting for a moment. "Anyway, here is my number. You can call me if you like." Janet placed a small sticky note in my right hand.

"Thank you." I never figured that Janet would be so kind to me and especially now. I could only imagine what she and her children must going through. She had her faults, but she was right about one thing: we were both grieving for Carl.

"I am sorry for you and Bentley." Janet rose and reached for a hug. Feeling dumbstruck, I watched her walk away. Maybe I was wrong about Janet. Although her sincerity had me puzzled, I conceded and reached for my purse and put her number away.

I lay my tired and weary body across the bed and closed my eyes. The sounds of chatter accompanied by the clanging of dishes and the familiar aroma of mom's old coffee pot crept in. Then I heard a voice all too familiar.

"Hiyee! How can I help?" Our neighbor, Rita, came by just about every day, lending a hand as was needed and tending to my tears. She would find me if I was resting high upon the moon, that Rita. She was bold, willful, determined, and very blunt. She didn't care if she offended or befriended anyone, that's just how she was. Her favorite phrase being, "but I mean no harm" as she told you just how she felt about things. She was real. When the news reached her household of Carl's death, she was on the phone calling mom and tracking me down. On occasion, she could be a little forceful. However, she was always a reliable friend in times of need.

Knowing she'd be on the porch with the smokers, including my mom and Keithan, I could hear Rita's distinctive laughter floating in the air. As she snuffed out her last cigarette, she opened the kitchen door and asked Natalie for a plate. Her voice loud and affirmed, I knew she would find me with that plate. I could hear the thud of her boots on the wooden floor as she eagerly made her way towards my room.

"Knock, knock, you already know who it is," she spoke cheerfully. "How ya' holding up? I still can't fathom that this happened!" Her gaze examining me carefully, like a doctor searching for signs of life. "You know I love you. You've got to get up from this bed, Hope!" Her voice was now more commanding.

I nodded to Rita in acknowledgement because I knew her words came from a good place. Deep in her heart with all sincerity, offering generous hugs while extending a chicken leg and saying, "Eat dammit!" Her expression was so serious and intent. I knew I had to take a bite of the food, or she would stay there all night.

In all her glorious black locks, newly polished red acrylic nails, and starched denim Levi jeans; she was Rita Smothers, my neighbor and friend. No amount of money or material possessions could replace her sense of humor and genuine kindness. She was truly one of a kind.

After about an hour of sitting and reminiscing, Rita mentioned she had to go home and cook for her husband

Joseph. "Well, I have to go now. I love ya'll. I will be back tomorrow." Her way of putting us all on notice.

Like most of mom's neighbors, Rita was *good people.* Neighbors that were kind and hospitable, quick to support each other. Still, in all that goodness, they couldn't help but share the latest gossip circulating around town about Carl's death.

The rumors spread like wildfire, adding an extra layer of pain to our already unbearable situation. Every whispered word felt like a sharp knife, reopening the wounds in our hearts. Words that echoed in the silence of the night, taunting us and weighing heavily on our chests with each breath we took.

Until I lost Carl, I was unaware of people's cruelty. They engaged in casual gossip and spread it all abroad. A populous of twisted and manipulated truth that became something unrecognizable and wicked. The worst part was that no one cared. No one stopped to take note of the carnage left behind after the damage was done by whispering lips and meddling tongues.

Only those living in this hell knew what it felt like to be ripped apart and misjudged, mislabeled, and misunderstood. Putting an unnecessary burden on the families of the deceased. Creating another weight for us to carry on our already overloaded hearts. Again, I found myself asking, "Why Lord? Why Carl? Why does such evil live among us?"

When the dreaded day came to memorialize, we gathered to attend Carl's service. Bentley and I wore our best black suits and clung to each other for dear life. Hand in hand, we stood, looking at each other for a sign of hope and courage. I squeezed Bentley's tawny little hand and gave him a wink, as he looked at me intently while patting my back.

"It will be ok, Mom." My little angel, so precious and attentive. I knelt and gave him a smile.

"You're my little hero, you know that?"

With the sweetest expression he said, "I know," as he folded his arms around my neck.

The greatest blessing that I have ever received from my Heavenly Father. This adorable, tiny little person, with the biggest, most compassionate, benevolent heart of any human I'd ever known. I could not question God about why I deserved such a beautiful soul, but only to be thankful for receiving him. "The fruit of the womb is a reward." Feeling humbled as I held Bentley, I knew God saw me. He heard me, and He loved me. Mighty and gracious is He.

Our family congregated on a cloudy Saturday afternoon, with the pungent aroma of mom's honeysuckle and roses wafting in the air from her tiny cement patio. The dread was painted on everyone's faces as we exchanged glances, just waiting for someone to be the first to say, "Are we ready?"

Mom and Keithan were all dressed up to accompany Bentley and I to the funeral, with hesitancies, as they still felt some trepidation about our attendance. I couldn't recall Keithan ever dressing up for any occasion, so it was nice to see him looking all polished and handsome for a change. We'd become accustomed to his faded, holey jeans, eighties rock t-shirts, and thrifty worn-out sneakers as his daily attire.

Mom was a classic with her casual business style. She often dressed up for work or outings when she wasn't in her garden tending to her flower beds and roses.

"We need to get going, and get this over with," Mom sighed. I looked at Bentley, then at Mom, nodded my head as I reached for the car keys.

"You are not driving!" Keithan said as he took the keys from my hand and placed his arm around my shoulder. "Sis, you are in no shape, and we need to take a different vehicle to the funeral."

I didn't bother to argue with him and thought that maybe he was right. I certainly didn't feel much like driving anyway. The unknowns awaiting us at the funeral were daunting for everyone and expecting the inculpation that would greet us at the church doors was enough. Still, we were going to pay our respects to the man we loved and admired. Nothing would stop us from seeing Carl this one last time.

Keithan brought his truck around to the driveway and we all rode together as a family. My heart was pounding in my chest as I sat with Bentley, dreading the funeral. He just kept looking at me as though he wanted to make it all better.

We were hand in hand as we took the country drive some fourteen miles to the South. Bentley and I took deep breaths, in and out, the closer we got to the church grounds.

Looking over the seat at me, mom inquired, "Where are we sitting?" I could tell she was uncomfortable, but I was so proud of her bravery and more so of her loving support.

"I am sure they will seat us once we are inside, Mom."

Upon arrival, we could see cars lined up, one by one, waiting to park in the dusty church yard. The grounds were packed with people and the parking spaces were filling up quickly. Several of Carl's cousins waved us in, ready to escort us to the church steps. Some people stopped just to take in the sight of us driving past them. Others, gave us the side eye and held a stiffened posture with hands on their hips.

Rita was standing near the entrance, ready to get us in and out of the service as quickly as possible. As the truck came to a stop, I heard the doors swing open and felt a hand take mine.

"Come on. I've got you. Let your mom get Bentley." It was Rita.

"No, I want Bentley with me." I pulled Bentley closer as we walked up the steps and hugged several of Carl's family members. It felt as though we were being rushed inside by the Secret Service. Who was more afraid, them or us? Or maybe they were afraid *for* us.

Entering the church, I could see the faces of strangers with predisposed looks on their faces. I could feel their stares as Rita walked in with us.

"I need to seat you by the door," Rita said. But before we could take a seat, Mary motioned for us to move up front and sit on the pew across from her.

Mom walked up and whispered over my shoulder, "I don't think we should sit here. Let's move to the back. People are staring at us." I noticed the finger pointing and the wretched stares coming from the far-left pew.

"Mom, it is ok. We will be fine here." But the stares pierced through my body and ripped through my existence. Infinite stares that made me feel increasingly uncomfortable, as if I was being tried and convicted. And of what? These people did not know me and so many of them did not even know Carl.

"Please, let's get you out of here." Mom gave me that look. She sounded desperate in her plea.

"I am ok. Let's just get through this service. These people, with their ugly gestures, cannot do any more to me than has already been done."

I put my arm around Bentley and held him close as I wiped the tears from my cheeks. Mom agreed to remain put, but the look in her eyes was that of great despair. She sat next to Keithan and Natalie as they exchanged glances. My insides knotted up as I thought about the hours ahead of us. Having to sit there among the gawking faces was troubling. Somehow, I knew, with God's grace, we could make it through.

I could feel those tiny hands patting me on my back, little pats of love and compassion. I studied Bentley, searching for any signs that we should abandon our efforts and depart. That sweet little face staring back at me was saddened and despondent but caring and concerned. I kept thinking how this was not the life we planned nor how it was supposed to turn out for us. We were robbed of our happiness and our pillar. Bentley finally had a man in his life who would be a real provider, a teacher, a celebrant, and an emotional mainstay. This season in our life was just not fair.

As the choir sang and the eulogy given, I found myself praying for peace and protection. What was waiting for us beyond the service scared me and, by the behavior of the attendees, who could determine where the evil one sat. Which one was it? Were they staring and finger-pointing because we were the white family or because of the rumors they'd heard prior to their attendance? Carl's family had white family members, but I guess they didn't hear that one when they were down at the hair salon swapping gossip or at the barber shop talking it up. No man nor woman could resurrect Carl, therefore, no man nor woman could be judge or jury. Carl was gone and nothing would bring him back, nor could anything hurt him anymore. I thought to myself, this is as bad as it gets!

As the Preacher shouted about healing, heaven, and comfort, I was wondering where we could find our healing and comfort. It felt like no one could possibly understand what we were going through. But then I remembered reading about Jesus and how he was so greatly disturbed over the loss of his dear friend Lazarus that he wept. How could he do that if he didn't feel the same sorrow that I did? A comforting thought that held me together like glue.

The service seemed to go on forever and I could see Mary, Gina, Evan, Ivan, the grandkids, and several of Carl's aunts and uncles all in the front row. I could see Janet sitting with her children, all heads hung low in grief. She glanced over at me a few times and nodded her head. She seemed to check on us periodically from across the pews. An occasional half smile came from her face underneath the black lace veil that hid her tears.

Evan and Ivan were Carl's brothers, all closely knit. They both shared such a striking resemblance to him. Seated behind them were the extended family of cousins and other relatives from out of town that filled almost every row of pews in the middle of the church. I found it lamenting to look upon the utter agony that weighed so heavily upon them.

I glanced over at the casket several times but couldn't focus my eyes there long enough to take in the body that lay peacefully inside it. I kept my focus on Bentley, whom I never let go of as I cradled his small frame with my left arm.

As the service was ending, I felt a tap on my shoulder. I looked up from my tissue to see Rita standing over me.

"Come, walk with me! We are going to the casket and view the body, then get you out of here."

Keithan, Natalie, Mom, Bentley, and I all shuffled down the row. Bentley walked with Mom as Rita had her arm around my shoulder. The closer I got to Carl's body, the weaker I felt and the more I cried. I slowed and paused long enough to reach for Bentley's hand. I held it tightly as we turned towards the exit, my legs feeling weak and unsteady beneath me. Rita gripped my shoulders and shook me gently, urging me to stay alert and standing.

"Come on, keep moving," she urged. "Don't look at these people!" She kept us moving right on out the church doors.

"I hope you are satisfied now!" Spat an elderly lady as we exited the church. Rita stopped long enough to wave her off.

"Get you some business and get away from us!" Rita was furious. "Old bitty."

"Well if it wasn't for her—"

"Shut up! You don't even know what you're talking about!" Rita fumed.

I never let go of Bentley's hand as we swiftly made our way to our vehicle. Rita and two of Carl's cousins stood by as we climbed inside and drove away. I thought nothing could get any worse than that awful day.

I was aware that the sorrow and suffering would not disappear overnight; it would take time. I could only hope that eventually we would find some peace. The void was great and the loneliness greater, but the day would be behind us. Maybe soon we could move on with our lives. Piece things together and slowly regain a sense of normalcy with each passing day. What could I fear that wasn't already destroyed? But then, it began.

Chapter Five

After the funeral, we returned home to settle in for the night. Mom looked so sad as she gave me a long and distinct glance.

"I will deeply miss him. He was someone very dear to me and a truly amazing person. Such a shame." Shaking her head as she poured her evening cup of Joe.

Keithan chimed in, "You had yourself a good one, Hope! I sure do hate this happened."

I felt like dying right where I sat in Mom's brown oak dining chair. I knew the words they spoke came from a good place, but they also cut deeper than a double-edged sword. I could feel the water running down my cheeks as I rose with a deep breath and made my exit towards my escape room.

My hibernation quarters, my area of solitude, my refuge from the voices, a 10x12 bedroom with beige colored walls and brown wood flooring. In the corner was mom's white wicker chair, used more as a clothes rack than for sitting. The room was often where Bentley and I sat together on the bed adorned with a thick floral comforter and big brightly stuffed pillow shams. Mom so loved her flowers.

"Mom, when will you stop crying?"

Taking a hard swallow, I gave Bentley a hug and a kiss on the forehead.

"In time, Bentley. In time."

My son's gentle gaze was comforting as I struggled to hold back my tears.

"Let's get you off to the bath."

The warm glow of the bathroom dimly illuminated our quiet conversation. The sound of water running in the tub made a soothing symphony in the background. Bentley loved playing in the bath with scented bubbles as they floated freely into the air. He pretended to blow them from his hands as he gathered them one by one in his palms. To see any excitement on his face was tenderly soothing and to hear him laugh was an elixir to my sorrow. He was such a sweet little character.

After his bath, Bentley climbed into bed with his favorite brown teddy bear with the cute red bow tie and black fuzzy nose.

"Don't forget, ma, tuck Teddy in too." His big brown eyes shimmered in the soft glow of the lamp light.

"Now, how could I forget Mr. Teddy?"

I placed his teddy bear carefully next to him, its brown fur glinting with a smooth sheen. Bentley picked out his favorite bedtime storybook from the Book of Bible Stories, with all the bright, beautiful pictures inside.

"Read me the story about The Boys Who Lived Again." Bentley loved his stories, and he took such an interest in the Bible even at a very early age. I was amazed at how well he retained what he learned and read.

"You really like that one, don't you?" I gleamed.

"Yes, ma'am."

As I read the story to Bentley, I thought about how Elisha and Elijah, with Jehovah's help, performed life saving miracles. It reminded me of when Jesus resurrected Lazarus and how the scriptures speak of a resurrection right here on earth. It was a comforting thought and one that brought me profound tranquility. Comfort that I desperately needed at that very moment. I could see why Bentley loved it so much.

"Ma, that sure is a good story. Can you read it again?" With a content smile on his face, Bentley's eyelids were getting heavier by the minute. It wasn't long before he was resting.

While I watched Bentley sleep, I couldn't stop thinking about the story and about what Keithan said earlier. He was right when he said Carl was a good one. One of the best.

Carl's death was tied up in conspiracy theories and every week a new version or tale was being shared from neighbor to neighbor. The cacophony of never-ending speculations was exhausting. Life became easier for me to just stay at home and nearly give up on living. However, as bad as things were, I found that giving up was not an option.

Dealing with constant anxiety, the idea of trying to resume a normal routine was overwhelming. The mere thought of having to socialize felt unbearable. The whispers were out there, everywhere, and just the notion of it stressed me immensely.

News was spreading far and wide, but not much of it was the truth. And as the story goes, Carl was murdered because of his associations and whom he was dating. At least that is what got the popular vote.

The majority did not know me and had never met me. I was labeled by the event but not called by my name.

Between the death and the malicious gossip, it was a mortifying experience, to say the least. I could not fathom how people could just believe whatever they heard without question and run with it like carrying an Olympic torch to victory.

On both sides of the spectrum, the whispers of scandalous gossip continued with ghastly assumptions and sensationalized information. Although most did not know it was Hope Everly they were speaking of, their words still found me, and the injury was still the same. It was as if I had done something wrong, and already convicted. But the only thing I was guilty of was loving another human being despite our cultural and ethnic differences. Love is where you find it and often where it's least expected.

Even those that knew the truth never asked how we were coping with the scandalous rumors. Most days I just wanted to crawl into a deep hole and never come out again. My load was heavy, and my mind clung to the shrewd, cruel nature of others. I rarely slept or ate. I felt like, if I could disappear and never be seen again, the pain would go away, and the hell would go with it. But I couldn't do that. I had a son to love and support and shield from the haters and nay-sayers.

Bentley needed me to help him make sense of this life-changing occurrence. He depended on me. We needed each other desperately, and I wasn't about to abandon him. I just had to figure it out somehow. I had to find that faith.

Not only had I lost Carl, but I was front page news in everyone's gossip column and the latest dish on the social table set for conversation and ridicule. I made the street committee's community voice platform, in every beauty parlor and barber shop, every corner gossip clique, and weekend BBQ.

Indeed, details of Carl's death and his *girlfriend* were the talk of the town. It seemed like everyone was talking about *her*, intensifying my fear and isolation. The idea of knowing that I was on everyone's mind and lips, and the lies being generated, was just too overwhelming. How do you argue with the masses who already have their minds made up? How do you set the record straight? I was exhausted! And I was broken. What more could they do that had not already been done? I isolated myself from the world and I became deeply depressed. My focus shifted solely to Bentley.

I maintained enough mental clarity for Bentley's sake, as he was going through a difficult time. The loss had created a gaping emptiness in his life. An irreplaceable void that I could not fill. I tried my best to give him all that I could and with all that I had. We had to be strong and support each other if we were going to outlast our sorrow. My attention had to be on our safety and our health. Always alert and conscious of our environment. I prayed incessantly that the trauma did not forever scar Bentley. Prayer seemed to be the only thing I had left that I could rely on.

Bentley had his moments of reprieve, sharing laughter with mom and family. Keeping Bentley involved with fun activities as much as possible was remedial, but his favorite thing was his passion for the arts. With his remarkable skill, he could sketch anything. He poured his heart into his drawings that emanated the essence of his imagination. His artistic talents provided a therapeutic escape from the challenges and stresses of everyday life and brought him much jubilation.

Seeing Bentley find his joy in creative arts was like a bright light in a dark tunnel, casting away the shadows and bringing a sense of hope and brightness to our days. A welcome diversion from the dim and gloomy pit where I found myself fighting for a way out and back to the surface. The thoughts that I carried around every day, every moment, even in my dreams when I slept, were haunting.

For many, many months after, I would swear that I heard that apartment doorbell ringing. The same one from the night of my attempted murder. Just out of the blue, in my sleep, and at random, I could hear it so vividly. It was so real to me, verisimilar. Sometimes I could still smell Carl's cologne, perhaps buried in my palette, attempting to surface when my most profound thoughts became exposed. I could hear his voice calling me as if he were right there with me, poignant and evocative.

My mind was a mess, bewildered and tangled. I thought, "Ok, this is how people go mad." I feared closing my eyes because I didn't want to see or smell or hear, but then again, I did. The languishing was tormenting, but it was all I had left of Carl. Clinging to whatever memory I could and cherishing all that was not destroyed.

As I searched to find release from my season of grief among the bastille in which I was confined, a comforting thought came to me. It made me think of a different time in my life that I had forgotten about. In my youth, growing up, our family was in and out of ministry service. At one time, we were very faithful, until tragedy struck our household. Losing my brother Ridge in a boating accident had an indescribable and immeasurable impact.

Although we drifted from our faith during that time, the literature, and teachings from years of service to Jehovah were still present in our home. We could never completely forget about our Grand Creator, but life had a way of interfering.

In search of help, I reached towards the bookshelf and pulled out a Bible. It was slightly dusty from sitting unattended for so many years, but just touching it gave me a warm feeling. Opening to the inside cover, I could still read the name written in blue ink, Ridge Everly. Tears blurred my vision as a wave of emotion engulfed me.

Turning to the place marker, a scripture was under-lined in red ink, Psalm 94:19, "*When anxieties overwhelmed me, you comforted and soothed me.*' Through all the mad-ness, I knew in that moment that God had not forgotten about me. He heard me and He saw me. Through fervent prayer, I asked Him to hear me once more and deliver me from the evil around me. The more I prayed, the more I felt his protective cover cast over me like a blanket. I knew that without Him, I would not make it through the fire.

Every day, I set aside time to read and peer into the comforting words and prayers of David. The book of Psalms was my favorite. If ever anyone alive knew the pains and pressures of this world, it was David. Despite all his talents and abilities, he still made numerous mis-takes in life. He took the wrong path here and there, but because of his faith he overcame his enemies and found joy and peace. The two attributes I was desperately seeking, but seemed so impossible to achieve. I knew I needed to have faith, but first I had to find it.

My struggle with loneliness and heartbreak still left me longing for connection and money was tight. Being out on leave from work for an extended period and run-ning out of funds was adding to the strain. Bills were mounting into a stack as thick as a novel and every single one was past due. I was already digging into our savings, but I was thankful I had something to keep us going.

Month to month, a decision had to be made to pay a bill or feed Bentley. Although mom and dad didn't mind helping us if we needed it, we rarely ever asked. My independent nature wouldn't allow me to grieve them with my financial distress. They struggled most of their lives and raised five children. They owed us nothing but love. They found their way to the American Dream and somehow, I too would find my way.

Watching the sunset from mom's beautifully decorated porch I thought about how supportive my family had been during these dark times and sleepless nights. I also thought about how they probably didn't sleep much, as they also dealt with the talk of town. Life wasn't easy for any of us.

"Come sit with me for a while." Mom smiled as she walked past me, coffee cup in hand.

"Ok. Let me grab a cup of your special sauce." I suggested as she gave me a wink. I knew she just wanted some company in the quiet of the evening.

"Hope, life can be hard to navigate sometimes. It is what you do with the cards you are dealt that matters the most." Her words seemed to cradle my soul, each syllable offering a warm embrace in the cool night air. She had a way of expression like no one else I knew.

"Mom, I don't expect a rose garden but I never thought life would be so cruel."

"Sweetie, life can lift you up or tear you apart. The only thing you control is how you respond to it."

As the days turned into weeks since Carl's death, the months started disappearing. Bentley and I officially moved in with mom, choosing the security of family, recognizing it as the optimal environment for us. We packed up the last of our belongings and put most of it in storage.

"I think I have the last of the boxes." My words were tired and labored.

"Hope, where is Bentley?" Mom asked.

"He was right behind me."

Dragging along, Bentley walked through the gate and up the front steps, carrying two small backpacks full of clothes and his toys in tow. "Ma, I think Teddy and I will take a sketch break." His eyes all lit up with excitement, bright and luminous. My little helper. "Ma, where are we putting all this stuff?"

Gently touching Bentley's nose, I laughed. His curious nature bore a relentless quest for understanding.

"Let's eat!" Mom chimed in. She had an infectious energy about her, like catching fire.

"I am ready," Bentley confirmed.

"What are we having?" I loved to see mom in the kitchen.

"Well Hope, I thought we would have some spaghetti, I know how much you enjoy that." With a smile, she set the table and lit two candles, the comforting smell of garlic and tomatoes filling the air.

Mom and Bentley laughed at each other's jokes while mom explained to Bentley the importance of having meatballs in the sauce. I came to appreciate her patience with him and her nurturing nature. She was a caring teacher, always setting an example for someone else to follow. She believed in hard work and discipline but showered us with loads of love.

Mom appealed to the creative side of Bentley and the two baked cookies and bread, but mostly enjoyed working flower beds together. I could sit for hours just admiring their work and the fun they had doing it. Every day that allowed, those two were planting and decorating and planning for the growing season. They'd laugh and joke and plan out each detail, feeling the dirt and sweat on their skin. I couldn't help but smile as I watched them from afar, admiring their creation of beauty out of nothing but mere dirt and love. Tender moments that touched my heart in ways I'd almost forgotten.

A bond grew between us as we became a unit of people who had endured so much together. We could fill the air around us with memories of those we had loved and lost, but also with cherished sentiments and unyielding hope. We had each other but found the hardest days to be most challenging, struggling to move on with our day-to-day and lose ourselves in the seconds so the minutes did not grieve us.

Even a fleeting moment of respite was treasured, recognizing its value amid life's demands. We knew for certain; our lives were forever changed when the threads of time became entangled in the relentless march of reality.

Chapter Six

The seasons came and went, but winter brought a coldness that I couldn't ignore. The wind seemed to cut right through my coat and chill me to the bone. The cold made my body ache and stiffened, reminding me of another experience that nearly killed me. Carl would say, "Hope, you have to get back in the saddle sooner or later." I was afraid to get behind the wheel after my accident. But Carl insisted that I confront my fears, or they'd haunt me forever. I knew he was right. Just like I knew I had to re-enter society and pretend like nothing had ever happened to us.

Hiding away for eternity was not a viable option. I had to face the world, no matter the cost, but fear was alive and well and had rooted itself within me. I had bills to pay, and Bentley needed to see me moving forward, getting on with my life. I shuddered at the thought of him relinquishing his dreams and withdrawing from the world. I feared his contentment to keep his thoughts and emotions locked away. The life I envisioned for him was vibrant and full of endless possibilities without fear or limitation. But I had to take the first step out of my cage and step out on faith.

I took my tan leather-bound planner from my briefcase, with its gold embossing and double stitched edges. Staring at its rose-colored pages, the dates on the page were both inviting and overwhelming. Pondering, what would be my date of return to work? How was I ever going to decide? I'd been debating what to do for weeks, and the planner seemed to mock me with its blankness.

I took a deep breath and gripped a yellow chisel-tip highlighter and circled a date—Monday, one week from today. Staring at the bright yellow circle, I gave a determined nod. "I can handle this," I whispered quietly.

A loud ringing suddenly broke my concentration. Taken aback by the green pushbutton telephone sitting on the table, I quickly looked around to see if mom would answer it. The phone rang again, startling me. I took a moment to gather my thoughts before answering.

"Hello? ... Hello?" No response, just eerie silence. "Is someone there?" There was clicking on the line. Was the call disconnected? I hung up the phone in frustration and returned to my desk to tidy up. But there it was again. The ringing continued. I couldn't bring myself to answer it, frozen in place as my eyes locked onto the handset. Just as the phone stopped ringing, my mom walked through the door.

"Did you take that call?" she asked. My heart raced as I stood there, unable to move or speak. The phone rang again, and she answered with a cheerful greeting, only to be met with silence on the other end.

"Wrong number, I guess," she said with a shrug, but her voice held a hint of uncertainty. We both knew that it could have been anyone, and that realization hung in the air between us with a heaviness.

I took a deep breath, willing myself to calm down. It was probably just a telemarketer or a prank call. But still, my heart continued to race, and my palms grew slick with sweat.

"I'll get it next time," I said, trying to sound nonchalant. But my words were hollow, and we both knew it.

"Are you ok, Hope? You look pale."

I could only nod my head while still staring at the phone. What was wrong with me? Crazy. Yes, just crazy of me. My mouth became parched as I tried to swallow and slowly settled back into the small desk chair, returning to my planner.

The highlighter in my hand was dancing around in a trembling manner. My fingers shook as I tried to firm my grip, a nervous energy coursing through my body. I could taste the metallic tang of fear on my tongue, overwhelming and unpleasant. I rose to gather my accessories and march off to the bath, hoping to soak away the day's troubles and find an escape.

The evening rolled in like a velvet curtain, thick and dark, with sounds of thunder in the distance. The rain tapping against the window caught my attention and became oddly comforting. I closed my eyes and focused on the sound of rain, letting it wash away any lingering stress or worries.

As the rumble of thunder grew louder, I let out a resigned exhale. I stepped out of the soothing warmth of my bath and into a plush absorbent towel. My eyes briefly took notice of the woman in the mirror, in all her curves and edges, slipping into a blue of bedtime attire. I wasn't sure I even recognized her anymore or if the mirror just reflected the woman I'd become.

Shaking loose and free from the confines of its clip, my chestnut brown locks cascaded down my back. Each tangled strand coiled and effortlessly danced along my shoulders. While my body eagerly sought refuge under the soft covers of my bed, my thoughts of the week ahead were lingering. The thunder grew louder, lulling me into a peaceful and deep sleep.

"Hope, come with me." A hand stretched out towards me, but I could not see the face. I reached out to touch the hand against a bright and blinding light.

"Where are you? Where did you go?" There was no one there. The light was growing dim when suddenly the phone rang.

"Hello?" Silence greeted me. Then ...

"I am watching you!"

With a sharp gasp, my eyes flew open. The sudden intrusion startled me awake from the abyss of the night. I sat up in the bed with labored breathing. The phone continued ringing until mom answered, "Hello? Is anyone there?" After a moment, she hung up and went back to bed. "Damn pranksters!" She was frustrated. "Who would call at such a late hour?"

Exhaling, I realized I was somewhere between a dream and reality. I closed my eyes but the uneasy feeling in my gut wouldn't go away. I tossed and turned before giving up and heading off to the kitchen for coffee.

The next day was quiet, and mom kept Bentley and I busy with chores and gardening. She didn't mention the late-night caller, but I could tell it was on her mind. Her usual warmth was muted by a lingering preoccupation. There was a weight in the air, a tension that clung stubbornly. My thoughts were complex and confused between the night caller and the strange dream that left a wrench in my stomach. The air was thick with a sweet scent while a gentle breeze blew through my hair. But despite the idyllic setting, there was a sense of foreboding that hung over everything.

The week seemed to fly past us and Monday arrived, leaving my palms sweaty, and my heart racing. A million different scenarios played out in my mind, as it felt strange to be returning to the office. With a pile of overdue bills that needed attention, the promise of a paycheck was my motivation to push through my nerves. The stack of bills seemed to grow larger every week. A daunting sight, the mountain of white envelopes with threatening letters and staggering dollar amounts.

The scent of paper and ink emanated from the bills, a reminder of all the money that I owed and couldn't pay. It was a sickly-sweet smell, laced with stress and anxiety that I wanted to set on fire and forget they ever existed. I was buried in a hole, six feet deep, suffocating in a claustrophobic tomb of financial burden.

Impelled to put on a brave face, trying to pretend that I wasn't dying inside, I steadied myself and entered the building. It was frightening to go back into a world that drove me into seclusion and tucked me away inside myself. Each face that met mine felt intimidating and scrutinizing, as if they could see right through my façade. As if they knew the turmoil I was trying so desperately to hide. Hiding the pain and hiding from the unknown that may lie in wait for me.

Inside the office, the rustle of papers, the tapping of keyboards, and the murmur of voices all blended together into a dull hum. Beneath all the noise, I could still hear the whispers directed at the corner office where I was stationed, along with the side eye glances that came from gossiping colleagues. The water cooler talk was frequently about Carl's murder, and one coworker in particular expressed agitation for her safety with me being in the office.

"I mean, really, Hope! Why did you even have to come back here?" Eyes rolled and heels clicking, she made her way to HR to file a complaint. Wow! Talk about cutting me to the core.

"You do realize, it's tough seeing you among us, don't you?" Another one barked.

I often found myself lost in thought, contemplating whether people truly comprehended the profound effect their words had on others. It was a delicate dance, with every word carrying the potential to heal or harm. How I wondered if people were aware that casually tossed out phrases could ruin someone's day or even their entire life. How brazen!

I brushed off her comment and continued my work as if it didn't bother me. No one knew I was bleeding out inside, still grieving and fearful, trying my best to carry on and hold my head up. Those words from her just ripped me open and rather than let her know, I stepped away to let go of the force that was bottled up, contained but ready to explode; to release the pressure of the anguish that I carried heavily upon my heart.

I washed my face and pulled myself together, pretending that I wasn't falling to pieces. To those on the outside of my life looking in, I appeared to have it all without a hair out of place. Strong, brave, collected.

"I don't know how you do it, keep yourself going," some said. Truth be told, neither did I. I just knew that I didn't have a choice. Nothing could stand in the way of protecting Bentley's well-being. Nothing and no one. Ever.

I reminded myself of my responsibility to raise my son and to love him and protect him. If I didn't have Bentley, how easy it would have been to slip away into the darkness. To disappear into the night like vapor fading as it blends with the wind, vanishing out of sight. Swallowed up by the breath of emptiness, ceasing to exist at all.

Despite my constant desire to give up, I knew Carl would never have wanted that for me. While the thought of escaping to an unknown place, where I could live without fear or pain, seemed like the better option, where exactly would that be?

Pain became a constant companion, waking me every hour of every day, permitting no escape. The smile I wore was my disguise so people wouldn't know the secrets I kept hidden. I found it was easier to smile rather than to divulge what no one else could ever understand.

I lived inside my bubble, my own personal reserve and fortress of self-contained existence. This was a place where I could be in control and escape from the pressures of the outside world. In my bubble, I could be whoever I wanted to be, without having to explain or justify myself to anyone. This preference for solitude wasn't just a choice—it was a necessity. It was the only way for me to cope with the constant barrage of negativity surrounding me. In my bubble, I didn't have to worry about my safety or my sanity.

For the outside world I had created a daily routine. I drove straight home from work with no stops in between, afraid for the darkness to catch me out. If I needed gas for the car, I strategized on where to stop for fuel. Making sure the station was brightly lit and parked where the attendant could easily see me. I scanned my surroundings, hurriedly paid the attendant, and left. I was frantic.

On the highway, my mind continually wondered if the demons were still lurking, waiting for an opportunity to try to get me. Was there someone waiting for me up the street, around a curve, hidden in the night's shadows? My eyes were constantly surveying the area and rearview mirror.

I couldn't expel the eerie sensation that clung to me like a silk scarf in a strong wind. It was like a persistent itch on the back of my mind, an intangible yet undeniable presence that lingered with each passing mile.

My palms were clammy, and I could feel my heart racing as I drove down the empty country roads, surrounded by darkness on either side. Every mile that stretched out before was a race against time. Then the time finally came.

Headlights. Appearing out of nowhere. They seemed to get closer and closer. Riding my bumper. Matching my speed if I sped up or slowed down. The driver blinked his lights twice. What did that mean? I increased my speed, rounding each turn in a fury. The car that ensued was unrelenting. I pushed my car faster. Tires hugging the road's edge, barely missing the shoulder. The darkness of the night surrounded me as I sped down the road at over seventy miles per hour. My headlights cut through the gloom, illuminating the curve ahead. The smell of burning rubber filled the air as I slammed on the brakes, only slowing down enough to make the sharp turn, barely keeping my car on the road without losing traction. Rounding the curve, both vehicles pushing their limits, down the hills and up again. Blinding beams in the rearview mirror became obscuring to my sight. The road ahead blurred beneath the tires as the chase unfolded with a deafening intensity. And just like that, the car was gone. It was as if it vanished into thin air.

Several more miles passed as a sense of unease and fear gnawed at my stomach, making me feel as though I was being watched or followed. My thoughts were on

Mary, remembering how she made me promise her I would stay inside after dark and go straight home from work every day.

"Don't you let dark catch you out, baby," she said. She meant well, but her words seemed to heighten my perturbation. It created more urgency and panic within me. And now I feared living.

Safety was a luxury I could only find within four walls, and even then, my mind raced with fears of bullets piercing through the doors or windows. The slightest knock at the door made my heart race and my palms break out in a sweat. I harbored suspicions towards anyone I was not familiar with.

My fists forever clenched, determined to keep my tears and apprehension hidden behind my facade. But I wasn't the only one grappling with a sense of vulnerability. Bentley was also scared. Both of us were grappling with the challenges of our daily existence.

Trying to keep Bentley uplifted, I always assured him. "We are fine, it's okay, nothing to worry about." He seemed to accept my words as comfort and formed a little smile, his tense body relaxing and arms resting by his sides.

I wanted to always keep Bentley with me, never letting him out of my sight. Even sending him to school made me anxious, but it was something I had to do. The maternal instinct within me fought to shield and protect my son from any worries or fears about his mommy. I could feel his concern for me as he clung to my side with nervous energy.

Despite the weight on my heart, it was my mission to keep a loving smile on my face whenever Bentley was around.

Our lives were full of limitations and tightly confined within our tiny little familial cocoon. I gave Bentley as much adoration and praise as I could, creating the most encouraging environment possible for him. But I wondered, how long would we have to live a life of reclusiveness? We were always looking over our shoulders out of fear, scared to go out of the house. How long before we got our lives back? If we ever got them back.

Each day felt like an eternity, as if time had halted in its tracks and was barely inching forward. It was a never-ending cycle of monotony, where every moment seemed to stretch out into months. The hurt was still ever so painful, still fresh in our hearts, unrelenting. Establishing a sense of normalcy proved challenging, yet I strived to infuse Bentley's days with as much joy and activity as possible. He needed more than family time to elevate his talents and help him develop his social skills. While we felt confined by our apprehension, Bentley still had to go to school.

I understood Bentley required privileges that would foster his personal development in real-world environments and continue to build his confidence. He needed to expand on his scholastic and positive peer influences tailored to his needs as a gifted child. Which moved me to enroll him into a class for gifted children. He had an IQ of 150, and that was a gift and a curse. Bentley learned differently than his peers, and he consistently needed arduous tasks set before him. This made his desire for imaginative experiences more demanding.

Bentley craved adventure and couldn't help but marvel at how effortlessly my mom seemed to churn out fresh concepts. Her mind was a constant whirlwind of creativity.

"Granny, where do all your ideas come from?" he asked, curiosity getting the better of him. She turned to look at Bentley, her eyes twinkling with amusement.

"Oh, they just come to me, darling," her voice filled with whimsy. "I have a universe of treasures inside my head, just waiting to be explored." Bentley couldn't help but laugh at her zestful response. She was great with Bentley like that.

While mom was most jovial, she was no stranger to grieving. Over the years, she had experienced the pain of losing many loved ones. As I watched her battle adversities with unwavering bravery, I couldn't help but admire where she got her strength from. Was it from the strict upbringing she had? Or perhaps it was the hardships she faced early in life. Whatever the source, clearly, she possessed a fierce will to persevere. She inspired me with her strength, and I drew mine from the model she set for me.

Every time Carl's name came up, a bittersweet smile would form on Mom's face. The grief in her eyes was revealing with every tender word she spoke. I knew that she, in all her greatness, was still grieving the loss of two sons, two parents, and a husband from years past. I watched her struggle with death, but I also saw her rise every day and find a reason to go on with life. She was amazing to me! I somehow felt like, if she could do it, then so could I.

"Bentley, you best wrap up today, son. Let me help you get your coat on." Mom carefully guided his arms through the soft, woolen fabric.

"Ok, granny." He willingly put each arm inside his coat sleeves.

"I packed some soup for lunch." Mom packed a small thermos in Bentley's backpack.

"Don't forget the PB&J, granny."

"I wouldn't dare. How can a child survive this cold without PB&J?" She and Bentley laughed.

"Yes, ma'am. It is colder outside today, huh granny?" Mom nodded.

"Yes, and you don't want to catch a cold."

"No, ma'am. No fun being a sick child." He replied as he slipped on his gloves, pulling and twisting until they fit snugly over his hands.

Winter was rough, with its bitter cold, and bustling, windy days. Frosty mornings with iced-over windshields, waiting for the car to warm so we could get Bentley off to school. With the cold and the continued isolation, my everyday routine of protective custody was becoming depressing.

Day in and day out, same ole routine, always looking in the rear-view mirror to see if I was being followed and checking the turns for parked cars on the roadside, anticipating sniper maneuvers. Observing the cars beside me at every red light, taking notice of the occupants, and always in a rush to get in before dark and back into hiding. It was madness.

Bentley and I sang songs in the car on our morning and afternoon drives. It was our way of creating some fun and distraction in our otherwise monotonous routine. He liked it when I sang along with Mariah on the radio, knowing his momma couldn't carry a tune but still made us feel good, nonetheless. It didn't matter if we were off-key or completely out of sync. We just sang and laughed and let the music fill the car. Bentley would squeeze my hand and give me a big smile.

"That was awesome, Mom," he'd say. I knew that these were the moments we would always remember and treasure. No matter what, we had each other and our cheery car concerts to keep us going.

Bentley was so precious, and I enjoyed my loving child infinitely. He was so astute. I marveled at his intelligence and inquisitive nature. Having always been advanced for his age, he was very gifted in his academics, demeanor, and artistic talents. I marveled at his rare and genuine solicitude for people.

Despite the overwhelming sense of emptiness I felt, God's provision filled me with strength and joy. There was no doubt that He blessed my life when he gave me a son.

"I sure miss the summer months." Mom wrapped a shawl around her shoulders and pulled out a cigarette. We dreaded winter and longed for the warmth of the summer season. The air outside was a pale shade of blue, as if it was trying to mimic the hues of the winter sky.

The trees were barren, their branches stretching out like skeletal fingers against the cold, grey horizon. A season that always seemed to sneak up on us in the South, with its unpredictable patterns of morning frosts and warm afternoons. This year, however, proved to be one of the coldest on record, with even the hardiest of Southerners bundling up in their thickest coats and scarves.

Back inside our cozy home we found refuge from the biting cold. The aroma of hot cocoa filled the air, thick and comforting, as we huddled around the fireplace. Our mugs were adorned with fluffy marshmallows and sprinkled with cinnamon, a decadent treat on a chilly day.

"Hey, let's have some of those famous gingersnaps you love to bake up, mom," I said. Her eyes lit up with the thought of it.

"Hope, that is a wonderful idea!"

We loved to spend the cold evenings by the fire. We'd read a good book or simply sit in silence and watch the flames paint flickering shadows on the walls as they spouted a gentle, soothing melody orchestrated by the symphony of burning wood.

"I think tomorrow we should have some of granny's famous beef stew," Bentley added.

"Sounds yummy!" I winked and smiled at mom while wrapping Bentley in a blanket. We settled in for a cozy evening, reveling in the warmth of family and the memories that I wished I could bottle up for safekeeping and live in those moments forever.

As the night drew on and Bentley grew tired, we said our goodnights and headed off to bed. A bittersweet feeling washed over me as I lay in the darkness of my room. Tomorrow would bring a new day, and with it, new challenges. But in all the hell that overshadowed us, we would always have each other.

Chapter Seven

S pring came, and it was comforting to feel the warmth of the sunshine, to smell the budding of trees, and to hear the birds sing out so joyfully. God's creation is a marvel.

The birds embark on life's journey even after they lose their saplings, fending for themselves among the predators, and foraging for food come rain, snow, sleet, or shine. They survive, knowing what it's like to be targets, dodging bullets, and predators, avoiding danger, and trying to stay alive. They know how to search for something, whether or not it can be found, yet they carry on, day after day, week after week, month after month. Birds live in survival mode and yet they thrive.

As I observed the graceful flight of the birds, I realized survival was becoming my greatest skill. Although I was hurting, I was also searching for healing; not knowing if it could be found. I longed for wisdom and restoration, determined to discover the way towards forgiveness, and yet I wanted vindication. I knew I needed to find my path to redemption, peace, and freedom from the confining emotions that bound my life and chained my happiness.

I needed a new perspective on life, and I prayed for deliverance from the demons that sought after my soul. I believed that with enough faith and time, somehow, there was a way out of this hell that seemed to never end. But just how much time? It was as if the intricacies of time tugged at the edges of my thoughts.

If only the emptiness would leave, and life be restored back to the way it was. Becoming resilient was what I sought most. I wanted to be like the birds, able to sustain and thrive. Each day carried an additional weight of absence, and each season brought poignant reminders of loss as time took on a different hue draped in shades of grief. A delicate sway between moments and memories in a world that somehow felt altered and inexorable.

My heart kept telling me to just let God take care of things. He is the healer and the Redeemer. All my struggles and worries were already known to Him; He saw them with His omniscient gaze. He also knew the perpetrators and their motives, and He would not let them escape unpunished. I just needed to surrender my burdens and trust Him and let him fight for me. I needed to find my faith. *For He is the potter, and I am the clay.*

Just like the new season of Spring, time was getting on. The month of April, with all its glory, was also the hardest month for us. April marked one year since Carl's death and the weight of grief was a laden cloak resting on our scarred hearts.

As if to mock us, nature continued its unstoppable march forward. Bentley was rapidly growing like a weed, sprouting towards the sky. His height increased every day and his limbs stretched out further. His growth reminded me of the fleeting nature of time and just how quickly it slips away. His laughter, his boundless energy, his innocent outlook on life, a reflection of simpler times. If only Carl could see the fine young man Bentley was becoming.

All hyped up and ready for the warmer weather, Bentley enjoyed playing with his cousins outdoors beneath the relaxing veranda that stretched the length of their summer cottage. His gleaming bright smile brought light to my life every time I saw it. To see him play with other children, laughing and dancing with moments of joy, was soothing and filled my heart. The landscape was serenely calming and peaceful as a gentle breeze blew now and again.

I enjoyed sitting on the porch with my mom in the evenings where we would talk about everything and nothing. The warm glow of the setting sun wrapping around us like a cozy blanket. Mom's presence was like a balm to my sapped spirit, and I treasured every second spent with her. The pleasant company seemed to help me keep my mind focused on happier times and less on how much I missed Carl.

Though impossible to let go, I kept pushing myself to find something positive in each day and in each memory, I had of him. I fought to reclaim a life like I once had, but the concept seemed distant and foreign, something I had long forgotten.

Every day felt like I was living a life that wasn't my own. Numb, lonely, sometimes angry, depressed, out of sorts, confused, almost depersonalized. Who was I? A mother, a daughter, a friend, a broken grief-stricken shell of a woman, and a shell is what I felt like. A mere existence. But I was alive.

My mind dared to explore questionable thoughts. Why kill Carl? Why was I spared? But as quickly as the thought entered, I pushed it away. I wasn't to question such things but rather be grateful for my life and focus on my blessings and responsibilities. These were profound thoughts that both troubled and humbled me. It was this humility that fortified my relationship with Jehovah, and it grew into more of a reliant refuge and comfort for my weakened spirit.

I had daily conversations with God and approached Him with thankful and patient affection. It was those daily conversations that kept me from going off the deep end, into a deeper and darker place of no return.

In my humility, I came to value the tiniest of things such as the birds: how their songs became a symphony to my ears, and the blades of the grass a vibrant carpet beneath my feet. I marveled at the leaves of trees, firmly attached to their branches and the trickle of water from the nearby creek, the sounds of its gentle flow calming my restless thoughts. It was in these moments that I felt most at peace, sitting on the side porch that lazy hot summer, silently praying for guidance from a higher power.

In my weakest moments, He gave me the strength that I could not find on my own. That strength was my ally, my constant companion, always by my side. Even so, the sorrow seemed destined to follow its own course. Leaving me wondering how much more time before the grief moved out and allowed me to move on.

The ups and downs and sleepless nights were frequent. It was like being on a roller coaster of emotions, sadness with a slow ascent, followed by a sudden, heart wrenching drop, leaving echoes of melancholy along the tracks. The nights were my battlefield, where I faced my inner demons and recounted my regrets. Waking up in cold sweats, reaching for Carl, seeking comfort and consolation in his familiar embrace, only to find an empty space. But as always, the night offered no answers, only more questions. When would I ever have the answers?

The days became shorter, and the leaves began to fall. I had been sitting at the kitchen table, staring out the window in a daze when my mom's voice snapped me back to reality.

"Hope, you have mail. In fact, here is a letter addressed to you."

Mother placed the letter on the counter and then went back to preparing dinner. The envelope's elegant shade of lavender caught my attention. It was a color that made me think of spring and new beginnings. I slowly pushed my chair back and walked over to the counter, my hand hovering over the letter for a moment before finally picking it up. I noticed the envelope did not have a return address. I opened it slowly and unfolded the paper inside. There was a faint scent of lavender, almost like the sender had pressed real flowers into the page. The few words written in neat cursive were simple yet cryptic: *Dear Hope, I just wanted you to know that I am thinking of you on this day. My advice to you: be careful.*

"Who is it from, Hope?" Mom asked with a hint of curiosity in her tone. I hesitated, not wanting to reveal too much.

"Umm, just a friend." I smiled hoping to dismiss the question and the weight of the unmarked letter. I quickly concealed the envelope and slipped it into my pocket, wondering who could have sent it and why? A flash entered my mind of the night the headlights appeared out of nowhere and then disappeared again. It was an image I could not forget. The feeling nagged me in the background of my thoughts.

"Dinner will be ready soon. You'd best wash up." Mom was sure to see my worry if I wasn't careful. She could not know about this. Whatever was happening, it was mine to deal with.

The season came and went, and it seemed like our lives slipped away. A year of nothing but emptiness and living in fear, not knowing if one day we would leave home and never come back again. A year of searching for the first day of the rest of my life. An empty chair at the dinner table, a face missing from the family gatherings, a voice missing on the other end of the phone, and a hand missing that I could never hold again. And yet, a murder still unsolved. Who was out there?

The cryptic letter kept me on guard, and I questioned if it was all just a prank. Every physical encounter with another human made me wonder if they were the mysterious sender. Every greeting, every exchanged glance became a potential clue, and the air was thick with uncertainty. The boundaries between friend and foe blurred as the letter had become a catalyst for a heightened state of alertness, leaving me to decipher the riddles hidden within the fabric of my everyday interactions.

No one knew what it was like just to get through each day pretending to be copacetic. Hiding behind a smile as a mask to hide the pain, appearing to go on with life undisturbed. It took all my strength to keep up appearances, concealing the constant turmoil within me. It was just enough that no one would know the veritable hell I was living inside of myself. The cryptic letter was haunting me. I felt like the shadows had eyes and they saw my every move. There was nowhere to hide.

"You have a visitor, Hope." My coworker, Brittany, announced.

"Ask him to come in, please." I looked up from my desk to see a tall slender man in a three-piece suit staring at me. His eyes never left mine.

"Hope Everly? Not sure if you remember me?" His stature was commanding.

"Yes. I do remember." I watched as he closed the door to my office and pulled up a chair.

"My name is Albert Thomas. I am with the Bureau."

"The Bureau? Of course." My insides felt weak.

"I am investigating your finance's murder and I have read the report on your attempted murder." He sat there staring at me awaiting a response. I nodded as we exchanged glances.

"Ms. Everly, I will be frank. Your life may still be in danger. You really should consider leaving town." I blinked a couple of times before I could drum up a sentence to address his cold response.

"Sir, I cannot just leave town. I have nowhere to go. My family is here. Why do you feel that way?" I pushed a stack of papers away from me and leaned into my desk.

"There are some things that I cannot discuss with you. I can only urge you to think of your safety." His body language became tightening and purposeful.

"Wait! You walk in here asking me to leave town, but you can't tell me why?" I shifted my posture slightly and folded my arms.

"Look! I get that you may feel safer with your family around but with everything that has happened to you, don't you think you need a fresh start?"

As much as I wanted to argue his point, I couldn't. However, I simply couldn't uproot myself and Bentley and go trekking to the unknown. Where would we go?

"Think about it. Here is my card. If you should need me, call me. Anytime day or night."

I took his card and shook his hand. Maybe I should have told him about the letter and the phone calls but if I did, he may put me in protective custody. I just couldn't put Bentley through any more changes.

"Thank you. I appreciate your stopping by today."

Detective Thomas stood and walked out of my office just as quickly as he'd entered. I wasn't sure how to process the information. Maybe I should have told him about the letter at least. Could I trust him?

My coworkers looked on in suspicion and I could feel my skin crying out to run for the front door. Their whispers were echoing about, and I felt my anxiety bubbling up. Why did Mr. Thomas have to show up here?

I could hardly wait for the end of the workday so I could escape from the constant drone of typing and phone calls that filled the air. A symphony of tension and immediacy rested on my shoulders. My own forced laughter and polite responses to coworkers was suffocating my own emotions.

Watching the wall clock, I anxiously awaited my escape to break free from the office and get home to Bentley. Living isolated with no friends, no social outings, no relationships outside of family. What a life, and yet it was mine. Always asking myself, 'How did I get here? Would it ever change?"

I remember Carl being so proud of me for landing the sales position at my job. "I knew you could do it, Hope!" His words still singing in my ears. Would he be proud of me now? Would he live life like this and be taunted by the unknown? Would he trust this Detective Thomas?

The sense of injustice clung to me, settling in my bones like a constant throbbing ache. It had been more than a year since Carl's death and the lowlifes responsible still roamed free. I wondered if the ABI, with all their resources and expertise, would ever catch them. Would we ever have closure? I struggled to come to terms with the fact that justice might never be served. It seemed that the police had hit a dead end in their investigation and there were no new leads or developments. With each passing month, the void of losing Carl ate at me, leaving me more adrift and incomplete.

As I watched Bentley's growth, it became more evident that living in fear was not a sustainable option. The longer we stayed in hiding, the more Bentley would be consumed by it. We had to start living again, stop hiding away and come out of our shell. It was time for some positive change.

Bentley and I spent our mommy and son time watching movies, reading, or playing games together. He would entertain me with his sketches, and I loved to admire his drawings of people, architecture, and Bible characters. Bentley, so selfless and giving, thriving, but also struggling. Slow to make new friends and reluctant to socialize at school. If he was going to continue to heal, he had to have the best support system that I could provide for him. He needed a higher level of instruction. But where would we find that?

Sitting with my head down, thinking over my frustration, I heard Bentley's footsteps coming down the hallway.

"Mom, are you busy?" His voice sounded lifted. I turned to meet his enthusiastic approach.

"No, I am done for today." I pushed my work aside and gave Bentley my undivided attention.

"Good, because I wanted to tell you about a new teacher that will start at our school next week." He placed his backpack on the table and pulled out a letter.

"Ok. Let's hear it."

"She is very nice, and I like her already. She said that the students with special skills will be interviewed and considered for placement in a new class that my school will be offering. You must meet with her for more specifics. I have a letter."

"Wow. Sounds very interesting." Taking the letter in hand, I heard mom come in and close the door behind her.

"Bentley, I will read over this letter and see about meeting with your new teacher this week." The letter was very long but one word that leaped off the page was GIFTED.

"Is Bentley getting a new teacher?" Mom looked over, trying to read the letter I was holding.

"Seems like it and this may be the opportunity I have been searching for to get Bentley some additional instruction."

"Wonderful! That child needs to be at a higher level of academia. He is incredibly smart!" Mom smiled as she fired up the pot with her favorite blend of coffee beans. We sat for a while, sipping from our stone wear mugs, as we reminisced on the good times and how much we missed Carl.

"Do you think they'll ever get em'?" Mom asked.

"We can only pray, mom. Cases take time."

"Apparently, a lot of time!" Her voice expressed enough frustration for both of us to share. It was spine-tingling to think about the malice, the abuse, and the bizarre behaviors.

Memories that haunted me, clinging to my skin like a second layer. It is true what they say, sometimes you never know, until you know.

Chapter Eight

REFLECTIONS

S ummer brought with it a flood of memories along with lots of humidity. As I drove over the infamous bridge admiring the cerulean blue sky, my skin steeped in the balmy, sunny day. I reflected on the abundant memories that Carl and I had together.

Immersed in life like we were the only two people living in this big blue world. I still remember Carl showing up every day to see me like I was the only woman in the world for him. He looked at me so intently and lovingly, melting my affections in one great big smile. Mom said he was dashing. She grieved for him like he was one of her own children.

As much as losing Carl hurt me, it hurt even more to see the sorrow in her eyes. She fought the pain just like she fought everything else, with a strong will and a determined spirit. She told me once that if it wasn't for her faith, she never would have made it. I remember her telling me, as if it were yesterday.

"You must get up and put a smile on your face every day, Hope. Keep yourself industrious. You must make your own happiness, sweetie."

Her strength and joy, despite all her trials, were endless. She had figured out the formula for survival. That's when I realized, no matter how difficult, we must learn to endure life's most unforgiving circumstances. Gather up our inner strength and pray for wisdom to march on with what's left of our integrity. Develop a stronger will to live. It was undoubtedly the hardest thing I'd ever had to do. Life was teaching me, and God was protecting me. It was up to me to make the most of what I was given.

Life was beating me up, but I had not forgotten Carl's constant encouragement for my success, like a coach to an athlete he never wavered. He always saw my potential and pushed me towards my dreams. Now I needed to do the same for Bentley. If I gave up and allowed the darkness to win, where would that leave him? I had to overcome the obstacles in front of me, mostly in my head, and not allow the present circumstances to dictate my decisions. But my struggles with depression remained a hidden battle that I chose to fight alone. And fight, I did.

Refusing to let the darkness overtake and cripple me, I prayed constantly. I spent two years searching for my faith, only to realize that it wasn't God that left me. He was always present in my life. He woke me up every day and gave me courage. All I had to do was ask. It was by means of my faith and the will of the Father that I kept going. My strength came from Him and from knowing that Bentley needed me, my brave little boy.

Would we be in Texas living an enchanted life by now? Carl as a business owner living his dream, me a prominent executive, and Bentley a renowned artist? Would we have the six-figure incomes, the affluent HOA neighborhood, and the comfort of our achievements? We would never know. All I knew was we had to keep our heads up and our hopes high. Keep holding to the expectation that soon someone would be held accountable for Carl's murder.

As I examined the events of the past, I thought that there was a definite connection between Carl's murder and my attempted murder. Was it more about me than Carl? Maybe my mind was just toying with me. Maybe I was just reaching for straws and searching for answers, desperately trying to make sense of the senseless. Maybe I just wanted to find closure to move on and show Bentley that the world is not so terrible after all. Whatever it was, I couldn't lose sight of the future that Bentley deserved to have.

Very early on, after Bentley was born, we were blessed to have my parents to step in and coddle Bentley, filling the void so early in his life. They provided a home and helped us when we needed it the most. They became our compass, steering us through uncharted territory, and their amity was a constant anchor, grounding us in all our uncertainty. I was especially thankful for my dad and his nurturing embrace he extended to Bentley.

Dad was a soft-spoken, humble man, full of sagacity, tall and tan, with thick, dark curly hair and brown eyes. He loved his snap on Western-style shirts, khaki work pants, and country music. Whenever Dad worked on a project, Bentley was always by his side, handing him tools and offering his tiny but eager input.

Bentley was dad's pick and he referred to Bentley as his little buddy. The two were almost inseparable as they gardened together and spend countless hours side by side. Dad showed Bentley how to grow things and how to tend to the land. Lessons that went beyond gardening, as Dad modeled hard work, responsibility, and compassion.

My father's presence lifted some of the burden I carried as a parent myself. Bentley needed a male role model and companionship as our financial hardship forced me into jobs that were laborious and dirty, long hours, shift work, double shifts, factories and mills. I was away from Bentley more than a mother should have to sacrifice her time. Places that were taking me nowhere but to a paycheck, sometimes two jobs just to make it. A single mother's struggle is real as she fights a battle that leaves no room for weakness and no room for surrender.

I remembered how desperately I longed for a change in my life. Always dreaming of a fulfilling career that would afford me more time with Bentley. That longing brought the desire to return to school and earn a degree. The thought of balancing work, college courses, and raising a child seemed impossible and far from my reach. So, I kept working, taking different jobs, one better than the last and each one increasing in pay. I was working my up the ladder, at least, that was the plan. And that ladder began with humble beginnings. Only this time it was a managerial role at the local convenience store. I felt like I was finally getting ahead and creating a good life for me and Bentley.

But like a dark cloud looming on the horizon, I would meet someone who would change everything. Someone that came into my life *before* I met Carl.

His name was Alex Cooper.

Chapter Nine

I remembered Alex Cooper's face so vividly. How he lit up a room with his infectious smile and big glassy brown eyes. They'd crinkle at the corners as his teeth gleamed in the sunlight. Standing tall at 6'1 and 190 pounds, muscular, well groomed, and always friendly. His job as a supervisor at the local woodyard allowed him to drive luxurious cars and live quite comfortably.

Everyone spoke well of Alex and had nothing negative to say about him. He was a hard worker and kept a small circle of friends. He projected a bad boy air about him but also a purposeful allure. His speech measured and assured; he was unmistakable when entering a room.

Alex was a regular customer at the store where I worked and stopped in everyday, sometimes twice a day, and three times on weekends. Always friendly and gazing at me until he finally worked up his nerve to ask me out. We exchanged phone numbers and began dating shortly after. It was nothing serious at first, just phone calls and lunch. A few months later, I met his family and close friends. Everything was going great, even better than expected.

We dated for a few years before Alex changed careers and became a logistics commodity manager. He was motivated to move up the tax bracket, and I was excited that he finally landed his dream job. He was bouncing off the walls with excitement. It wasn't long before we were engaged and moved into a newly renovated farmhouse of his father's. These were exciting times for us. But, as time went by, there were red flags, disturbing things I noticed about him.

Alex would disappear for hours, and his attitude became cynical and arrogant. Regardless of the situation, everything was funny to him, even sad things, which became very strange. If I questioned why he disappeared for periods of time he would become angry. Sometimes he didn't come home from work until the next day. The more I asked, the more agitated he got. What was he hiding?

"Where do you disappear to, Alex?" I would ask as I watched his body language.

"Stop asking me all these dumb questions! When are you going to get an actual job?" Alex became inflamed.

"I have a job, Alex."

"At a gas station?" He smirked.

"It's a convenience store, Alex!" I spat back.

"You need to make some real money and pull your weight!" He seemed so frustrated and demanding. I could sense his dissatisfaction with me. His eyes seemed to pierce right through me as he sat and swigged his beer from the bottle. In an effort to keep the peace, I began searching for employment opportunities.

After a few weeks I landed a job at Walford's Furniture. I worked as a cashier before advancing into the cash office, then later advancing into sales. This was a far better opportunity with a higher wage than the convenience store. I was excited about it, but Alex still seemed indifferent. He rolled his eyes and popped his gums as if I worked in a sewer. Nothing was good enough.

Between his disappearing acts and his mood swings, my curiosity grew by the day. But I dared not to ask. Life seemed to move along as if we were going through the motions. Strangers under one roof. It was becoming clear to me that we needed to part ways and move on from each other. However, the fear of having the conversation with Alex held me at bay. I knew I had to tell him, and I had to do it soon.

One of my biggest faults was looking the other way too often. Giving too much of myself especially the benefit of the doubt. But the more I observed Alex's behavior, the more it became evident that I didn't know Alex Cooper at all. His behavior made the hairs on the back of my neck stand up and my gut turn and churn until the relationship began sapping away at my joy and hope. My life was beginning to resemble a Lifetime movie, with no way to bail out of it.

Alex became creepy and he would stare at me with an evil, unsettling look, then smack his lips and twist his mouth. Pretty soon, he became aggressive and abusive. Finding every fault with me that he possibly could, even down to the smallest of things. Either I couldn't cook to his liking, or I didn't fold the sheets properly. I didn't sweep the floor well enough, or he didn't like the way my clothes looked on my body. Something was always wrong with me.

Alex was a dominating, controlling person. His posture was always rigid and imposing. His chin raised with confidence and his arms crossed in a stance of authority. His piercing eyes seemed to radiate power and control. He towered over me, his broad shoulders and chiseled jaw exuding dominance as he criticized my every existence. He isolated me.

"You don't need friends. You have me."

I felt the weight of his control, suffocating and imprisoning me. Instead of allowing me to have friends, he always insisted that I stay at home, tucked away neatly from the outside world. He had me right where he wanted me.

Alex was sneaky and also a cheater. He thought he hid it well. Lying about his conversations with other women as if it wasn't noticeable. He even became fixated on a particular woman on our block, rushing to the door every time he heard her car pull into her driveway. His eyes followed her every move, studying her like a bird of prey. There's was no doubt that his behavior was questionable with an air of mystery. Suspicious.

One hot summer night, Alex came home from the club, late as usual. He had an unsettling look in his eyes, one like I had never seen before, almost evil. It was like I was looking at a total stranger. He approached slowly, gritting his teeth, and then began hitting me, slapping me repeatedly, his fists striking me all over my face and body, knocking me over the bed and onto the floor. He held me down, beating me black and blue all that night. The more I said stop, the worse it got. My neck, face, back, and arms were severely bruised. My lips were swollen and cut open. The edges of my fingernails were jagged from fighting back. My body hurt to breathe.

The next day, I had to cover myself with makeup and a turtleneck just to go into work. Despite my best efforts people still noticed, and it was mortifying. Stares and whispers from coworkers and customers hurt almost as much as the beating.

I desperately wanted to get away from Alex and never think of him again, but I was terrified. He had threatened to kill me if I ever left him, and he promised he would dispose of my body where it would never be found. I felt completely trapped. Where was my escape?

Alex later said how sorry he was, and it would never happen again, but I wasn't sure I believed him. He wasn't at all what I expected or should have been involved with. I thought I knew him, but just who was he? How could I get out of this mess? Just leave, I thought, so many times. Just walk away. But what if Alex was serious about killing me? I was afraid. So, I stayed.

After Alex became all apologetic, things seemed better for a while, but I wondered every day if he would ever hit me again. I prayed that it never happened in front of Bentley and thankfully it did not. I prayed every day for a way out. Every day I begged God to help me. Show me the way or make a way for me to leave without him coming after me. "Please, Jah! Help me. Save me before it is too late."

I became skilled at hiding the bruises, the cuts, the welts from the abuse, but some people still knew. They would stare, their eyes full of care and pity, but they never questioned. They knew, and I knew they knew, and yet we all pretended that everything was fine. It was a dance we did that became a delicate balancing act. I would plaster a smile on my face, and they would nod sympathetically. We all pretended that I was okay, that my life was just like everyone else's. Deep down we all knew the truth.

The scars on my body and the distressed look in my eyes were impossible to ignore. I continued to pray daily for strength and courage, but it just seemed hopeless. I thought I was never going to get out.

Attending to Alex's requirements, I did everything he asked, but he never found contentment. Exhaustion weighed down my body as I struggled to keep up with his ever-changing moods.

Every day I would go straight home from work and cook his meals even if he never came home for dinner. I cooked and cleaned and catered, but nothing I did was ever good enough. When he got mad, he threatened me, and when that wasn't satisfying enough, he beat me.

One night, while getting ready for bed, Alex struck me with such force that I feared he'd broken my jaw. Over what? Nothing. Just him coming home late with that weird look in his eyes again. What was he into? Did he have an obscure past? Why couldn't he just leave me alone and let me go? I did not have the answers, nor did I know who I could turn to for help. No one would understand. No one could help me, or so I thought.

One Saturday evening while doing laundry, I noticed some plastic in Alex's garments. I reached into the dryer and pulled out a square package that had been opened and was missing its contents. I was stunned! "What the—?" After several minutes of staring at the package, like it was going to speak to me and give me all the details, I realized Alex was a liar and a cheater. How could he not only cheat, but be so dumb as to leave the scabbard wrapper inside his clothes?

I felt like I was going to explode with mixed emotions of hurt, disbelief, shock, and anger. I moved from the laundry room to the bedroom to confront Alex with the package.

"What is this?" I asked as he looked surprised and blankly stared back at me.

"What is that? Where did you get that from?" His eyes wide and filled with guilt.

"It was in the laundry with your clothing."

"I meant to throw that away, and before you jump to conclusions, Hope, it's not mine," he laughed. Laughed! Like, what is so funny, dude? He came over to me with a smirking look on his face. I thought, "Wow, is that the best you can do?"

"If it's not yours, why is it in your clothes, and I'm assuming your pocket?" Presenting the pants from the dryer, he stared at them before looking back at me.

"Well, I like I said, I was supposed to throw that away for a buddy of mine."

The smirk grin on his face I was telling. I mean, who does that? Who keeps a scabbard wrapper for their friends? I stared at him with disgust.

"I don't believe you and I am not taking this crap! Do you think I am that stupid, Alex?" My heart was racing and my hands shaking. Alex moved in closer within inches of my face.

"So, like what are you going to do about it, trick?"

At that moment, I knew the gig was up. I mean, I knew I had to get away from this man and out of the relationship as quickly as possible. No woman should endure such disrespect and belittlement. He was like a disease. A cancer. Slowing eating away at me from the inside out.

"Alex, I think we should end this! I will not tolerate your behavior, nor will I live my life this way!"

I turned to leave the room when I felt a sharp pain in the back of my head. My feet left the floor and my back slammed with a loud whack against the brown ceramic tile. Alex grabbed my hair and pulled me backward into the room. Slapping me in the face with such force that my jaw went numb. Then another slap across my head.

"Shrew, you gonna leave me? No one leaves me!"

Another blow to the face. He grabbed my throat and squeezed. It felt like all his strength was being applied and there was suddenly no air. I couldn't breathe! The room was getting darker, and I was blacking out.

"The last person who tried to leave me didn't! You better think twice about crossing me!"

After a few minutes, Alex released his grip from my throat as I desperately gasped for air. I couldn't get enough air fast enough. I thought I was going to die.

"Don't let me hear of this! You better not tell anyone, or I will kill you!" Alex shouted as he stormed out of the room and then out of the house, slamming the front door. I slowly rolled over on the floor as every part of my body burned from the force of his hands.

Feeling my face with my fingers, checking to see if I still had teeth, the swelling started to set in. My face was throbbing, and my nose was bleeding, trickling down onto my shirt. I reached for the bedpost to pull myself up and then stumbled over to the mirror. As I looked at my face, I could see the puffiness around my eyes, the redness and abrasions, and then my eyes fell upon my neckline. The hand impressions of his fingers were like tattoos on my throat. With every swallow, the pain intensified. Was he going to kill me? I truly believed he would.

I reached for a towel to wash my face, to erase the tear marks from my red, inflamed cheeks. Standing there in misery, looking timidly into the mirror at the once familiar face reflecting back at me. I no longer recognized her. Who are you, I thought? I recalled the demeaning words that Alex yelled at me while striking my face, blow after blow, feeling terrified and hopeless.

This was not the life I had dreamed of or even thought I would be living. Why did I stay this long? Why didn't

I see what kind of man Alex was from the beginning? I mean, his family even seemed a little off. I knew his brother, Art, abused his wife, Lily, but Alex wasn't like that, right?

I couldn't raise Bentley in that hopeless situation, and he couldn't know about the abuse. I had to cover myself until I figured a way out. What was Alex's trigger? Did I just provoke him and shouldn't have? I needed to think. He made me question every action I took and every syllable that flowed from my lips. I became powerless.

The only beacon of hope I had was prayer. I asked God to intervene and give me guidance and strength to endure until I could see the way out. Most of all, pray for the safety and safekeeping of myself and Bentley until it was all over. Would it ever be over?

My daddy always said, "Everything that glitters, ain't gold!" My sweet daddy. So wise, if only I had listened to him. He never liked Alex. Why couldn't I have seen what dad saw? I was still young and dumb, trying to find my way.

The path I was walking was leading to nowhere and I had many days to reflect on the should of, could of, would of. I came to believe that we rarely see through our emotions until they become our tragedy, and in those moments, we bleed. I was ready to stop bleeding. I was just waiting on time.

Alex was an imposter, a liar, and a manipulator. He had secrets I would never learn, nor did I want to know about. I was living with the devil and the demons were after me, seeking my life, anyway they could get it. The fire was hot, but my redeemer and savior would deliver me. So, I believed. He was all that I had left.

Alex came home later that evening and acted just like nothing ever happened between us. He had one of the biggest smiles I could ever remember painted across his face. I wondered what was so amusing to him? Was this a game to him? How many times had he played that same game before?

My mind kept racing with thoughts like a speeding train, thundering down a track with no brakes in sight. I had so many questions about this man that I thought I knew. A man I thought was incapable of inflicting harm on others, especially me. Why did I believe I was an exception at this point, or ever for that matter?

In that single moment of clarity, I realized that a man's true nature is unchangeable. No one is exempt from his malicious intentions, as they are ingrained in his very being. Whether a lover, a friend, or a committed soul, no one is spared from those dark and twisted ways. Twisted and sinister.

My situation was critical, and the realization was that I had to woman up and own my tragedy. I also had to pick my time to vacate, to get out of the horrid mess that had become my prison, and hopefully at a time that would not result in Alex hurting me. Not knowing the when or how I would escape, the wait was the hardest. My secret had to be kept hidden; my parents, above all else, could never know.

In my head, I was trying to gather my escape plan, mapping out every scenario, when I heard Alex shout at me.

"Hey! Fix me some dinner, please."

"Really?" I thought. Why bother at this point with sincere words like please? I was damaged beyond the words of please, thank you, I'm sorry - if I ever heard that one, and forgive me - I doubt it. Instead of subjecting myself to any more abuse, I rose from my seat and walked to the kitchen. I knew I had to play nice, until I figured this thing out. I had to go along with Alex no matter what. Only God could help me now.

The weekend was over, and Bentley arrived home after having a great time with his grandparents. Taking a quick glance at my reflection in the mirror, I was pleased with my newfound skill of concealing. Thanks to makeup, I could effectively mask the bruises and not draw any attention to them. The swelling had also decreased thanks to frequent ice packing and elevated resting.

Bentley skipped into the house and didn't seem to notice. We sat and talked about his visit with his Papa, his way of referring to my dad. His eyes lit up every time he spoke about their adventures together. He made my soul smile.

Bentley brought such joy and distraction to my dark world. If only I could keep those precious moments I shared with him locked away to enjoy forever. He deserved a world with no chaos or uncertainty, one that provided him with stability.

"Mama, I love you!" Bentley so lovingly expressed as he wrapped his little arms around me. This child was my saving grace. "I love you too, Munchkin!"

I watched as Bentley played with his stuffed toy, Brookes, his favorite toy of all. He loved to watch his Brookes videos that were very educational and taught Bentley things like counting, ABCs, how to treat others with respect, and how to be a good friend. I was sure to provide him with anything that brought him joy and taught important lessons in life.

Bentley wore nice clothes, ate good meals, had a beautiful home, and went to a wonderful school. He wanted for nothing and out of everything that I provided, I just couldn't seem to provide him with a good father. That deeply pained me. I sat and cried about it frequently, and

I truly felt as though I had failed him. Even though, I did everything I could to be a nurturing mother, I still felt like I wasn't giving him enough. I could see that he, as a son, needed a father, always present in the developmental and influential stages of Bentley's life. Sure, my dad filled in and loved Bentley, providing him with a role model, but I knew Bentley still longed for his father each and every day. Although, Levard wasn't the father he should have been, I was determined to give Bentley every chance for success, even if it meant making sacrifices. And that journey did not include Alex Cooper.

I had to get out before it was too late. I'd lay awake at night wondering what evil lay beside me and what dark secrets Alex was hiding from me. I prayed to be set free from the hell that covered me like dirt on a grave. To rise and walk away without fear of retaliation or dying. Just to sleep again, peacefully, without clinging to a tear-stained pillow or feeling my skin hurt to the touch from his abuse.

Somehow, someway, someday, God was going to make a way out and I was going to take it. He was going to give me the courage to be fearless in the moment and enough so, that I could run. Run fast and far and free.

I believed.

Chapter Ten

I t was a cool November day with the sun peeking through the alabaster wood blinds covering the large bay windows in my bedroom. I could smell the coffee brewing from the kitchen as I entered the hallway and shuffled my feet on the brown ceramic tile.

"Good morning, Beautiful!" Popping up from around the corner with a crimson red coffee cup in hand.

"Alex! I didn't realize that you knew how to make coffee."

"I don't." He grinned intently as he poured the hot liquid from the pot. "Here, I made a cup especially for you."

A cup he brewed especially for me. Brewing coffee was usually my job. I woke up early every morning to make sure that Alex had his coffee before he left for work.

"Drink up, sweetie! I am running late for work." He leaned in to kiss my cheek as I pretended to sip from the cup that he prepared for me.

"Make sure you drink that!" His left eye winking and his mouth shining a few teeth with a sideways grin. I nodded with a slight smile as I starred ominously into the brown liquid, the steam from the cup rising up to kiss my face. Watching the swirls and patterns that formed on its surface reminded me of my own life, chaotic and unpredictable.

"I may be late coming home tonight. Board meeting. You know the story."

I sure did.

My eyes followed Alex as he walked out the door. I waited to hear the lock turn. Then rushed over to the window to see Alex as he casually strolled into the garage. He fidgeted with his key fob and his black leather briefcase for several minutes before climbing into his vehicle. He looked around suspiciously and paused for a moment, as if he were looking for someone, before keying the ignition and driving away.

As I watched Alex's Jag turn the corner, I quickly poured the coffee down the sink and ran to the bedroom. I began packing everything that would fit into bags and suitcases. I sprinted out to my SUV and immediately started throwing stuff inside it. I grabbed everything I could put my hands on and some essentials. I then ran to Bentley's room and quickly packed all his toys, clothes, bedding, and personals.

"Ma, are we leaving?" Bentley's small voice called out from behind me.

"Yes, baby! Hurry, help mommy get these things."

As fast as I could pack and load, I was sprinting through the house, slinging all that I could carry into my arms. All that I could stuff into the back of my SUV, cramming and jamming as much as possible. My heart was racing, and I was sweating profusely. I kept checking the street corner. Praying that Alex didn't come back before we could leave.

Then, I heard a motor coming. I looked to the corner for Alex's Jag. "Please, God! Please!" I whispered under my breath. The sound of the motor got louder and louder as it came closer to the house. I just kept peering at the corner, waiting for a car to come into view. The motor roared loudly as it got closer. If it's Alex, what will I do? I know he will kill me if he catches me. Just another ten minutes to freedom. I was almost done.

Staring at the corner, waiting. The sound of the motor grew louder and closer. My knees shook, and my palms became sweaty. I stood there thinking, if I close the hatch and go inside, would Alex notice anything? What should I do?

Watching and waiting for— there it was! A jag! Green like the one Alex drove, glistening as it rounded the corner. The motor had a rhythmic purr like a cat stalking its prey. And just when I thought I could die, it was Mr. Davis that lived on the next block. Sweat rolled down my face as I grabbed the back of the lift gate and steadied myself. The deep breath I was holding escaped my lips in a tremble. I ran back into the house and met Bentley dragging his tiny backpack down the hallway.

"Ma, I'm ready." Bentley announced.

"Ok, baby. Let me grab this last bag and we can go."

We loaded up the last of it. Leaving behind all the furniture that I bought with my hard-earned money. The sofa, the bedroom suite, the armoires, flat screens, dining set, and China. Everything that once meant so much to me but just didn't matter anymore. He could have it all. I just wanted out. I locked the door behind us and helped Bentley into his seat.

My heart was racing and pounding like a drum. I wished we could fly instead of driving, rising and soaring above the clouds out of Alex's reach.

Every turn I took, every corner, and every block, was frightening, looking for Alex to be anywhere and meet us on the road at any minute. Gassing the old SUV to get away as fast as we could. "Thank you, thank you, Father!" I shouted. I was scared to death and hyper-tense, but at least we were out. I never wanted to see Alex again as long as I lived. Prayerfully, that I lived.

Alex made his threats against me leaving and what he'd do to me if I did. But now it was done. I was terrified but free. What would be the price of my freedom?

My SUV came to a stop at an all-familiar place. Bentley rose from his seat with the biggest smile.

"Papa! Papa! We came to stay, Papa!" My dad looked at me curiously but didn't ask any questions. He helped Bentley out of his seat and took him inside while I unpacked the vehicle.

As I approached the porch, mom came out to greet me. She gave me that look like, well, it's about time.

"I hope it's ok, mom? We need a place to stay for a while."

Mom with her hands on her hips and her head titled to one side let out a sigh.

"Stay as long as you like. Have you eaten?" Her expression conveyed both worry and tenderness.

"No, not yet. I am sure Bentley is ready." I smiled at mom as she motioned for me to follow her.

"Your dad has a dish in the oven. You know how he likes to cook." Her gaze shifted to Bentley and dad huddled in the kitchen.

Mom gestured towards a door at the end of the hallway. The wood was a deep mahogany with intricate carvings and the room had the smell of clean linen.

"You can sleep in here." The room was small but cozy and was adorned with floral bedding.

"I like this room, ma." Bentley walked up behind us. Running his tiny hands over the bedding and pillows, holding Brookes with his right arm, and his backpack in tow.

"You do, do ya?" I tenderly asked as I noticed Teddy was peering over the zippered edge of his small backpack as if taking a peek.

"Yes, ma'am." Bentley's sweet little voice chanted with excitement.

"Good, let's get our belongings put away."

After getting settled in, we had brunch with mom and dad. Bentley went outside to sit with dad on the side porch so mom and I could talk for a bit.

"You finally had enough, I see." She said as she ran her fingers around the rim of her coffee mug.

"You knew?" My voice choked.

"Only a blind man couldn't see what was going on with you."

I just stared at her blankly. I couldn't believe she knew my secret and never said anything.

"He said he'd come after me if I left him," I whispered. Mom's eyes tightened.

"Hope, he can also go to jail or hell, his choice."

I'd never heard my mom speak words like that before. She said them with such conviction, and then she took another sip of her coffee and reached for my hand.

"Never let a man hurt you like that! My first husband thought he could hit me and get away with it. He found out differently." She squeezed my hand before turning back to her cup of joe.

"Did you get out before it got too bad?" I'd never heard this story before and looked on in shock.

"Not before he almost killed me, and I was pregnant."

"Oh my gosh, mom!"

As she took another sip from her favorite cup, adorned with brightly colored shapes and patterns, she winked her eye at me.

"He's dead now." Her smile frightened me.

"You mean he died later on, right?"

She got up from her chair as if she hadn't heard me ask and went outside to have a smoke. She just left me there to wonder. But I knew. My mom was feisty and animated, but she could do no harm. Still, I just sat there on the edge of her kitchen island, twisting on the stool that held my weight. Wondering. Did she—?

The antique Victorian clock that hung on the wall said six o'clock, and with every ticking sound I felt fear well up inside me. Alex was getting off work by now and if he went straight home, he would find us gone. He was going to know at some point that we left him. What would he do? I sat nervously staring at the phone.

The minutes felt like hours. Then I heard a noise that drew me into it like a solemn breeze of purity and innocence. It was the laughter of Bentley and his Papa. They had a close bond, like no other. Dad's eyes lit up whenever he looked at Bentley. His face softened with gentle fondness and pride. They were quite the pair to watch.

"Hope, come help me with dinner."

"Something smells delicious!" The aroma was making my mouth water. The yeasty scent mingling with the rich fragrance of southern home cooking was tantalizing.

"Pass me the bread pan."

Mom adored an old black, flat pan, with its edges all bent down, clearly a well-loved hand-me-down from generations past. She made the biggest, most delicious pan biscuits with that old treasure. Turnip greens, black-eyed peas, southern fried chicken, and peach cobbler rested on the brown oak dining table along with those beautiful, perfectly browned biscuits. So much love in every recipe. The aroma of the food permeated the room, bringing a sense of comfort and ease.

Sitting down to dinner, dad passed the platter around to each of us to take what we needed from it. In that moment, I felt such a sense of relief. The relief I had sought for so long but could not find. I closed my eyes and took a deep breath. I was home and I was safe. A feeling that no amount of money could ever buy. Priceless. Safety among good company was like food to my soul.

Cutting through the air, the ringing of the phone interrupted our bliss. The unexpected sound was unsettling as mom got up from her chair and walked over to answer.

"Hello?" She asked. Then listened.

"Let me speak to Hope!"

"Who is this?" Mom lifted her eyes towards me as her tone shifted abruptly.

"It's Alex!" I could hear his aggressive voice from across the room. Mom's face flushed with redness.

"She is not speaking to you, and you need not ever call my house again, Alex. Don't even think about bothering my daughter, either!" Mom's voice was loud and piercing.

"I just need to—"

"I don't give a damn what you need to! I meant what I said, and you don't want to try me! Hear me, Alex! You have done enough!" Mom hung up the phone and looked at me with fire red cheeks and exhaled.

"I could hurt him," she said. I couldn't say anything. I just looked at her with a pallid expression. Dad sat back in his chair and folded his arms.

"You may have to get a restraining order. You stay home for a few days and let him cool his heels." Dad was insistent.

"Dad, I must go to work," I replied softly.

"Well, you better be careful, because he is a fool."

I sighed at dad knowing he was right about Alex. I lowered my head in thought and pushed my food around on the plate with my fork. My bones told me that Alex wasn't done yet. If only he'd move on and forget about me.

My dad's words weighed heavy on my mind and bitterness filled my mouth as I repeated his words in my head. I knew he had a point. My leaving Alex was still too raw for me to assume anything. So, I called into work, honoring dad's request to stay home for a couple of days just to be safe. Besides, I wanted to keep my personal life hidden. I did not want coworkers meddling in my affairs. A few days off may do some good and give Bentley and I time to settle in.

The days passed with no sign of Alex, but I still feared the worst. Calls kept coming in at home randomly, with mom or dad always answering the phone. Each time the caller would hang up without saying a word. We knew it had to be Alex. He was still trying to make contact, hoping I would answer the phone instead of them.

It was the same, day in and day out, sometimes three or four times a day. Twice I answered. The dead air calls were creepy with heavy breathing that made my skin crawl. Every time the phone rang, I jumped and began shaking uncontrollably. I feared he may never give up and leave me alone.

"He's a coward! Doesn't he have anything better to do?" Mom vented her frustration. Dad was aggravated, but quiet. He wasn't a man of many words until he got wound up and then you best not mess with him. We were all tired of the silent caller.

"Let's go sit in our favorite spot." Mom motioned to me with that look of hers that told me she was over it. Over Alex and his BS and over dealing with the endless telephone conundrum.

As we sat in the breeze on mom's side porch admiring the hummingbirds and turtle doves that often came to visit us, the clouds rolled in on that overcast Friday afternoon. Mom with her smokes in hand and her legs crossed, one over the other, telling stories about the good old days and her parents' sharecropping. Something she loved to do just to pass the time.

Dad and Bentley were off shopping, picking up a list of items that mom asked for. Bentley loved to ride with his Papa, and it didn't matter where they went as long as he had his Papa by his side. They'd start up the old red farm truck and head out to nowhere. To Bentley, dad was larger than life itself, a sturdy and dependable presence that made him feel safe and loved.

As mom and I were relaxing and enjoying our sweet tea and lemon pound cake, she started with one of her stories. She'd just lit a cigarette when we heard a car drive up. Mom rose to look, thinking that dad may have made it back from the store with Bentley. But the look on her face told me it wasn't dad.

"Get in the house, now!" She dropped her smokes.

"What's wrong?"

"Go now, Hope!" Her tone startled me. I couldn't believe my eyes when I saw the green jag. Alex stepped out with a menacing grin on his face.

"Mom, come inside with me!" My breaths were labored.

"No, I can manage this."

"Mom, you don't know what he's capable of!" I pleaded. My insides were Jell-O.

"Get in the house, Hope. Now!"

Alex stepped out of his vehicle, dressed to the nines. He approached the gated fence with a gangster swagger. He stopped just short of the opening. Mom sternly walked up halfway and greeted Alex, never removing her hand from her pocket. Bear, her long-haired St. Bernard, faithfully by her side.

"Uh, I need to speak to Hope." Alex's eyes narrowed as he took a step closer to mom, his fists clenching at his sides.

"You need to get back in that green car and leave!" Mom anchored herself, firmly planting her feet.

"I need to see Hope!" Alex became agitated. His chest heaved with anger as he struggled to control the rage that coursed through his veins.

"You are not welcome here, Alex!" Mom's voice never wavering.

"What do you mean, I'm not welcome here?" Alex spat, his voice grated and menacing as he leaned into the fence.

"Get in your car and leave." Mom stood her ground, her hand still in her pocket. "Never, will you be welcome, Alex!" she said firmly. "You're a lowlife thug and you've caused Hope nothing but pain. You've abused her and damn near killed her! Somebody's gonna put a bullet in you one day."

Alex's posture stiffened and his muscles flexed as if he felt his blood boil at her words. Mom's face hardened. Bear's fur bristled up on his back as his growl rumbled.

"I will give you five seconds to get off my property. You can leave on your own or be carried off. Your choice." She never even batted an eye at Alex.

Stepping back, Alex grinned at mom and squinted his eyes; twisted his mouth and turned to retreat to his Jag.

He paused before getting inside, scanning the area, and popping his mouth.

"You cranky old Heffer, I'll be back!"

"Try me." Mom smiled.

From the kitchen, my hands hurt from gripping the window frame so tightly. I watched as Alex's Jag dug ruts in the gravel before he sped down the highway, tires screeching in protest. Mom kept her stance until Alex was out of sight before she turned to walk back up the driveway. I exhaled a long, shaky breath, feeling the tension release from my body. My heart thundered against my ribcage, almost deafening me as I tried to bring my presence back into focus.

Mom's face was stern with anger and worry creased her brow as she removed her hand from her pocket. She opened the kitchen door and stepped inside, crossing her arms over her chest. I moved closer so I could see her face.

"Are you alright, Mom?" A long pause held its position between us.

"Just makes me so dang mad! The nerve of that animal thinking he can just show up here!" She was livid.

"I'm sorry, mom." I fought back the tears. Mom stretched out her arms and gave me a hug.

"He has an evil look in his eyes, baby. He's dangerous. You need to get you some protection." I knew that was coming because mom believed in the iron.

"Mom, you know how I feel about that," I said. She released her arms and tugged at my chin.

"I understand, but you'd better start thinking about it, Hope. He is a different kind of evil." Mom left me with those bone chilling words and went out to the porch for a smoke. I stood frozen in the moment before joining her in the evening breeze.

Dad and Bentley returned about an hour later with the list of items mom sent for. Bentley was lit up like a roman candle, excited because he and his Papa went on an outing. He got to pick out a toy at Kensington's Toy Emporium. That was always his favorite store, and he could spend countless hours in there.

While Bentley and I played beneath the shade of a towering oak tree, my parents watched from the side porch. They were catching up on all the action that Dad had missed while he was away. His brows creased, and his lips pressed into a tight line, revealing his nervous tension about Alex's visit. Although he said nothing more about it, I could tell he was studying on it before he stood, arms folded and head high. His preferred stance whenever he was deeply disturbed.

The sudden ring of the phone sliced through the stillness of the afternoon, shattering any peace that may have lingered. We all looked at each other only to ignore the ringing. Mom walked to the mailbox and returned with several circulars. I followed her inside along with Bentley.

"You've got some mail on the corner desk." Mom pointed to the stack.

"It's likely just some unpaid bills." I winked at her. "You know one day, mom, I won't be poor anymore." She gave me the side eye.

"It never hurts to dream, baby."

Going through the mound of bills, I felt like maybe she was right. Maybe I'd never have the life I dreamed of for Bentley and me. We were barely scrapping by, and my job paid just enough to keep us below the poverty level. On the outside, it seemed like I had a picture-perfect life, always so elegantly dressed, nails manicured, and hair layered. Always a smiling face and personable on the surface. No one knew of the private hell or the financial struggle.

We Everly's shopped at thrift outlets when we could and budgeted every single penny. And even that wasn't enough to cover everything at times. We made do with what we had, the best way we could, and although we dreamed big, we met our needs before our wants. Life may have beat us down, but we were coming up, by the grace of God.

The days quickly became shorter, getting dark earlier than in those warm summer months we loved so much. Hot cocoa and warm fires beckoned for company as the evenings settled in. The darkness, certainly not a friend of mine, I feared with every sunset. Something I also began to fear was seeing a black SUV, always the same one, parked across the street from Walford's. It would sit with no movement for hours at the Tire Store. No one emerged from the vehicle, and it consistently parked in the mornings from 8 a.m. to 11 a.m. and then again from 3 p.m. to 5 p.m. I saw it every day while at work. Some evenings it would leave the parking lot simultaneously as my departure. I watched but it never followed me. Still, enough to keep me on edge.

"Hope? I need to speak with you." The store manager, Mr. Calvin startled me.

"Sure, Mr. Calvin." I rose from my desk and walked over to his office.

"Please, have a seat. This won't take long." He shuffled a stack of papers on his desk. "I have been watching you for a while and I noticed you are good at your job. I like the way you help our customers with furniture choices and room design and décor. However, I think you are better suited for a different position with this company. I would like to offer you a promotion as a buyer."

"A buyer, sir? Like a Purchasing Agent." I was stunned. He nodded.

"Yes." Shifting his weight around in the supple leather chair beneath his frame, he continued. "You'd be responsible for selecting quality decor that we sell right here in our showroom. Of course, I would still expect you to keep your current duties because you'd only function as our buyer once per quarter."

I didn't know what to say. Mr. Calvin sat still, waiting for an answer. I just stared at him before posing my questions.

"Would this require travel?" An uneasy feeling was working its way into the room.

"Minimal. You would also receive a pay increase that would put you at $40k per year."

"Wow!" My eyes widened in surprise and delight. My palms became sweaty.

"I know you can do this, Hope. I would not make the offer if I didn't believe in you." His words were both encouraging and intimidating. Could I really manage this new position and all its responsibilities?

"I don't know what to say, Mr. Calvin." I felt a sense of pride and validation wash over me.

"Say you'll take it," he said with a reassuring smile. Before I could respond, Mr. Calvin handed me a job description for the new position. My feelings shifted from initial thrill to nervousness.

"Where would I have to travel quarterly?" I needed to gather more information first.

"To our regional sales distribution centers, usually about one hour away." An hour away, on the highway by myself. My thoughts rambled.

"Sir, it's not that I don't want the job or need it, but I do want to think about it, if that's ok?" Silence hung in the air.

"Hope, do you know what I am offering you?" Mr. Calvin sounded testy.

"Yes sir... I do. It's just ...well, I need to talk this over with my family?" Mr. Calvin swiveled backwards. He stared at me across the rim of his blue optical frames.

"Ok, but I need an answer by the end of our fiscal quarter." His black suit jacket creased slightly, and his brown eyes bore into mine with a stern expression.

"Thank you so much!"

Walking out of Mr. Calvin's office, I released a deep breath. What an opportunity, I thought. I walked across the sales floor to the front window. There it was, the black SUV that somehow made me feel like I already knew the answer to Mr. Calvin's proposal. That subjective, self-contained, gut-wrenching phenomenal grind in the pit of my stomach that was telling me the black SUV was watching me. That feeling positioned itself to reveal that I would be prey for the kill if went on the road as a buyer. I needed the pay raise so desperately, but was the risk worth the opportunity?

Sitting at my desk, I evaluated the offer, contemplating, and weighing my options. I sure could use the pay increase. It was a tempting offer for sure.

"Hope?" A voice from the showroom reached my ears. I saw everyone gathering up their belongings. "It's go-time." Shouted a coworker. It was time to lock up the store, and I still needed to close out for the day.

I hurried to complete my paperwork and tidy up my desk. "Done." I chanted. The night crew were arriving and clocking in.

"Hey, you good?" The voice belonged to a tall and sturdy man, with deep-set eyes and a strong jawline. He wore a gray uniform with the company logo and a name tag that read *Jerry*. His voice carried a hint of mint, like he'd just popped a piece of gum. There was also a faint whiff of coffee lingering on his shirt.

"Yes, I am about to leave now."

The clock ticked ten minutes past closing when I headed to the side door for my car. Feeling inside my purse for keys, I paused and pressed my face against the window. There were no signs of the black SUV, it just disappeared. Pushing open the large glass doors to exit, a brisk breeze hit me in the face, blowing my brown curly locks from across my face.

"Where are you going?" The words stopped my heart. Fear paralyzed me.

"Alex!" Taking a hard swallow, noting his large frame standing before me.

"Did you think you could avoid me?" His eyes marked by evil.

"Alex, you need to leave." I backed against the wall. He moved in closer.

"There is no one around but us, baby," he said as he reached for my arm.

"Alex, please! Go on with your life and leave me alone." I tried to snatch away from him.

"Are you still stuck in this dead-end job? You know you need me. You had it good with me." That too familiar smirk curved up from the corners of his mouth.

"Alex, I was miserable with you, and you know you abused—"

"Abused!" He jerked my arm. "Don't you tell me I abused you, trick! You made me do those things to you. Besides, I was good to you." His eyes squinted as he inched in closer. "You asked for everything you got!" His voice graveled as he leaned into me.

"No, Alex. You beat me and you hurt me, and you damn near killed me. I do not want to be a part of that."

Bishhh. The door swung open.

"Hope! You alright out here?" It was Jerry from the night crew. Just in the nick of time. It was likely that he had spotted us on the security cameras. Alex released his grip.

"Jerry, I think I forgot something inside." I quickly darted towards him, gesturing for him to follow me. We entered the building together, and he locked the door behind us.

"Who is that, Hope?"

"Nobody." Shaking, I answered before leaving Jerry standing in the doorway.

"You are shaking like a leaf!" He followed.

"I just need to sit down for a minute."

"What are you mixed up in?" Jerry was persistent.

"It's a long story and I don't care to get into it." I lowered my head in shame.

"Do you need someone to take you home?" He stared at me with a demanding stance.

"No, but I appreciate it. And Jerry, please say nothing about this to our co-workers or Mr. Calvin." He nodded, but I wasn't sure if I could count on him to keep this a secret.

Realizing that I could not stay at Walford's all night, I phoned my friend, Miranda. She was a childhood friend and worked up the street at Mason's Grocery. I knew she wouldn't ask any questions. Making sure Alex was gone, Miranda trailed me home.

When my SUV pulled into the driveway, Miranda flashed her lights, signaling good night. I turned off the

car and sat there for a moment with my hands still on
the wheel. Listening to the engine ticking as it cooled
down, I exhaled. Just trying to calm my nerves before
making my way inside to greet Bentley. There was no way
I would bear the weight of this burden on my parents nor
tell them about the promotion that Mr. Calvin offered
me. They constantly felt worried about my safety and
their concern became a living thing. It pulsed in their
chests like a caged bird, its wings fluttering with fear
for their beloved. It was only when I finally entered the
doorway each night, did I witness the sighs of relief that
escaped my family's lips. With a gentle hand resting on
my shoulder, giving a warm, reassuring squeeze, I could
feel the tension releasing in their touch.

"How was your day, Hope?"

What could I say but, "it was interesting, mom." An
interesting nightmare.

Still needing a moment to reform, I entered the master bath and locked the door behind me. Sitting on the
edge of the tub before turning on the hot bath taps
and sluicing in a lather of honeysuckle-scented bath oil.
Taking in deep breaths of release as the steam hissed
up, scented with citrus extracts, dancing in mid-air, I
immersed myself in the comfort and healing of the heat.
It caressed every cell in my body, rejuvenating and pam-
pering the essence of my spirit.

I closed my tired eyes, which were filling up like
glassy pools overwhelmed with emotion, and submerged
my face beneath the liquid surface until I had to come up
for air.

"Ma, you in there?" Sweet Bentley. Knocking on the
bathroom door, looking for his mom.

"Yes. I will be out in a few minutes." I sat up in the
bath thanking God for being there, yet again, to keep me

in his loving care and for Jerry, coming to my rescue at just the right time. But also, for Bentley, always being that bright light on a darkened day.

I retired to the bedroom where Bentley and I read together underneath mom's antique Victorian floor lamp. Teddy Bear under one arm and his favorite book under the other. I watched Bentley as he lay so peacefully before drifting off to sleep.

As I tucked him in gently, kissing him on his forehead, I became full of emotion. The bliss of his sweet innocence, so precious and pure, filled me with uncontrollable sentiment. In all my troubles, I had so much to be thankful for. Although my world was upside down, I counted my blessings wherever I could find them. My greatest of all, was there in my sweet child.

Chapter Eleven

FLASH FORWARD

Alex was lethal memory. A past I was trying desperately to put behind me. His evil still taunted me, and the air held a sinister shroud of enigma, casting a malevolent veil on my surroundings. It was like each attempt to move forward was met with a fraught internal battle clinging to my every step. But a memory, is all that he was. I had moved on to a different place and time when I met Carl. A time of hopes and dreams and now a grieving reality. Carl was gone and a different kind of void lived within me. A void that no one would ever be able to fill.

Carl was on my mind as I walked into Walford's, ready to meet with Mr. Calvin and give him my answer. Carl had always been my biggest supporter, and I was certain he would be pleased with whatever decision I made. The pile of bills sitting on the corner desk back home reminded me of my financial tightrope, and the possibility of filing for bankruptcy as a last resort.

"Good morning, Hope!" Mr. Calvin seemed a bit irritated.

"Good morning. I would like to give an answer to your proposal." I froze. He held up his hand as if to say STOP.

"Hope, before we get started, I need to ask you about a particular incident." The look on his face was so revealing.

"Incident?" My voice was cracking.

"It's all on camera. I also spoke with Jerry."

That dang Jerry. Squealer. I knew he'd rat me out.

"Mr. Calvin—"

"No, let's talk about this! Do you have an issue going on that I need to know about?" Our eyes fixated on each other.

"No, sir. There is nothing for you or anyone else to know about. I had a little conflict with an ex, but nothing that impacts my work."

"Hope, I am not sure you are ready to be a buyer for us." His words startled me. He sat back in his chair and folded his arms.

"But sir, you were so convinced of my abilities and qualifications for the position." My head tilted to one side, I leaned forward. He bit his bottom lip. His hands clasped, betraying a tension I hadn't noticed before.

"I was mistaken." His expression was cold.

Rising from my seat with grace, the weight of our eyes locked, infusing the air in a palpable tautness.

"I see…. well, sir. I respectfully decline your offer. Thank you for the consideration." With a polite smile, I took only a few steps before Mr. Calvin interrupted.

"Hope! No more evening visitors, okay?" Turning to acknowledge my superior, I nodded my head slightly and walked away. Waiting for me outside the doorway behind a Bayhill buffet was none other than the snitch. I side eyed him as I walked past.

"Hey, Hope. Oh C'mon! Look, I don't want you to think that I snitched on you with Mr. Calvin or anything," He pleaded. I kept walking before turning to respond.

"Didn't you?" I gave a hard stare before gliding away from Jerry.

"Well, he was going to see the camera footage anyway, ya know?" His failed attempt to reason with me. I kept walking.

"Hope, come on now."

"Hope Everly, you have a call on line 2." The cashier's office was paging me over the intercom. I gave Jerry the side eye again and picked up the phone.

"Hello?" ... "Hello?" ... Breathing. "Who is this?" Nothing but dead air. I quickly hung up and walked away. I'd heard that breathing before.

"Hope Everly." Another one. Paging me from the intercom. I wanted to ignore it, but Mr. Calvin had his radar on me. I could see him stretching his neck, his head moving from side to side watching me from his office window.

"Hope! You gonna get that or what?" Bob Carter, over-achiever, and sales floor monitor. His posture was always upright. His chest puffed out with confidence, and his sharp eyes scanned the sales floor with precision. Taking a deep breath I moved closer to the phone.

"What is wrong with you today, missy?" Bob snapped. I reached for the handset and braced myself.

"Hello?" I answered abrasively.

"Hope, you need to come home." That voice was different.

"Hope, it's Rita. I am sorry, sweetie. Your dad has left us."

Dad suffered a fatal heart attack at sixty-three years old. My sweet and humble dad. I dropped the receiver and grabbed my purse.

"Emergency!" I shouted to Mr. Calvin as I ran out the door. I needed to get home to be with mom and Bentley. I now had to tell my dad's little buddy that his Papa was gone. God give me strength, I prayed.

Bentley's behavior became reticent and irascible. I could tell he was trying to make sense of his grief. I held him close as we read from the Bible together, seeking guidance and solace in its pages. Bentley had lost more than a grandparent, he lost a guiding companion, and a cherished teacher.

Without dad, our home felt emptier, quieter, and colder. Nevertheless, my mother endured the worst of the pain. She had been married to my father for over three decades, and now she was left to navigate a world without him. She seemed so out of place, as if she was searching for something or someone that had long since gone.

On those cold and barren days, I was oblivious to her struggles, but as time passed, hindsight brought clarity. Everything started to connect and fall into place. The pieces of the puzzle that lay scattered and confused in my mind formed a cohesive picture. I understood what she missed and why. I could almost feel the despair radiating off her, like a physical presence in the room. She wandered, her shoulders slumped and eyes downcast.

As she paced, a soft sigh escaped her lips now and then, giving away the heavy weight that seemed to burden her. I wished with all my heart that I could take her pain away and restore her light, but I knew deep inside that nothing could fill the emptiness that she felt. How can you fill an empty cup with no water?

Time became relenting by how it unfolded like the petals of a delicate flower, revealing all its beauty and imperfections, the bearer of sorrows and joys, in the staggering march of existence. It allowed for reflection and contemplation. Its echoes reverberating while its wilting petals reminding me of my reality.

Six long and grueling weeks passed, and the ringing of the phone became less frequent. But each time it did, my skin crawled like ants in an unsettling dance of dread parading across my body. I feared Alex would never truly disappear from my life. It all seemed so endless.

Then came a glimmer of hope as Bentley had just been awarded a prestigious art scholarship. He was over the moon with joy. He was full of exhilaration as he clutched the scholarship letter in his right hand. Sprinting down the hallway, his sneakers pounding on the hardwood floors. He burst into the kitchen where mom and I were preparing dinner.

"Mom! Mom!" he exclaimed, waving the letter in the air. "Look at what I got!" His eyes beamed brightly as he unfolded the crisp white paper with creased lines are crimped corners.

"What is it, sweetie?" Captured by his infectious joy, a warm smile spread across my face.

With Bentley handing me the letter, practically bouncing on the balls of his feet with anticipation, I read it out loud.

"We are pleased to grant Bentley Talleck a prestigious, fully paid, art scholarship for the current academic school year." My eyes shining with pride. "Oh, my goodness! Look at you, munchkin!"

"Bentley! That is so amazing!" Mom dropped her dish towel, reaching over me to squeeze his cheek. "You precious darling!"

"I did it, mom!" Bentley's heart hammered in his chest. His smile radiantly adorned his face.

"Yes, you certainly did, but then I knew you could." I wrapped my arms around him in a tight embrace cheeks swelled as his smile grew wider. "We need to celebrate. I will cook your favorite dinner tonight: chicken and dressing."

"Yippeeeee." Bentley couldn't contain his excitement. He needed this win in his life. I felt an immense euphoria for his achievements and flirted with the idea that maybe this could be the start of a brand-new chapter for us.

We set the table for a grand celebration. Our evening was fueled by unfeigned delight. Bentley spoke with more zest and enthusiasm that night than I'd ever seen in him. His voice was a symphony of vivacity, filling the room with a contagious energy. It was almost as if this win had lifted a heavy weight off his delicate shoulders and ignited a spark within his broken heart. His delight was a medicinal remedy for the sorrow that broke us down like a raging plague. The timing of his accolade was perfect.

He inspired me so much that I began to examine my own aspirations for achievement. I needed to be the example for Bentley to always strive for more. Demonstrating how aiming beyond the here and now can bring greater rewards with perseverance.

The path of fire on which we were walking was neither our home nor our destination. Out of the flames and into the ash, for us to rise, we first had to be the smoke. Smoke rising from the ashes of despair and disappointment, whirling up with a veil of escape, billowing with a smell of change, a cleansing, purifying scent that is soothing to the soul. Smoke rising with an air charged with electric energy, sparking embers of hope and passion, looking intently into the promise of better days that lay ahead. Rising up from the ashes of forlornness, spinning up with an air of freedom from the flames burning down our sorrows. When smoke rises, it dances into flight, gracefully transcending until it is free to fly. Bentley and I would become that smoke, and we would rise.

Our days of endless uncertainty and struggle seemed to be finding its closure. The strength I needed and prayed for was alive within me, burning with flames of hope that ignited my soul. Filled with the warmth of anticipation that washed over me like a gentle wave. I knew deep in my bones that it was time for me to leave Walford's and become the captain of my own ship. A steward of my own destiny. And setting sail for independence began with my commitment to furthering my education.

The dreams I had required credentials, so I braced myself for the unknown. A journey that required working long hours to support us, and to pay for what the Pell grant did not. My body was tired and weary, but my mind buzzed and hungered for success. A new life beyond the stagnated existence we had come to know.

I was all too grateful for the chance to liberate myself from the enduring cycle of abuse and pain that defined me for far too long. I set fire to the rain that was drowning me in unpaid debts and unmeasurable insecurities.

After four long years, I mastered the robust scholarly complexities to earn my Bachelor of Science degree at a prominent university. A mere and distant dream was now an achievement. A door had been opened to change on the horizon. The first person in three generations to graduate college.

"Hope, I am so proud of you!" Mom swelled with pride. With her enthusiasm bubbling over, dancing about like an effervescent fizz, she shared our news with everyone. This was a cherished moment she would always hold dearest.

"You did it, ma!" Bentley was ecstatic, beaming with joy.

"Yes, Munchkin. We did it!" Nothing could stop us now. We were on fire.

But where was Alex? He remained in the back of my thoughts like a repulsive stench. I desperately wanted to be free of him. Thoughts crept in like ghosts from the shadows. Never truly setting me free.

The black SUV was still stationed across from Walford's, and those unsettling calls continued to come in every few weeks. The caller ID always displayed as Unknown Caller or Private Number, intensifying the secrecy and discomfort surrounding the situation. And then there was the matter of the cryptic message that loomed ominously in my mind.

Each day I took notice of the black SUV and its imposing presence, giving it an air of mystery and danger. A portentous shadow in the otherwise bustling streets of our small town. The windows, thick and dark, like smoky quartz, and the body was sinewy and refined, that stood out against the brightly colored storefronts and vibrant displays. Each day I stood in the window at Walfords, gazing at the lonely presence of the black-on-black glossy dome. Who was inside it?

"Hope, can you catch the phone for me? I have a delivery?" Nobody but Bob creeping up to disturb my watchful eyes. He was always asking someone else to catch his calls when he was going to be out.

"Why not." I smirked, acknowledging Bob. He was such a pain, but at least he had a passion for his job and preferred the hands-on approach to sales and delivery. I could certainly admire that much about him if nothing else.

On the first and third of every month, the sales floor was packed with customers making payments and buying household decor. The cash registers jingled nonstop, the aisles were filled with chatter and laughter, and the store's signature scent of freshly brewed coffee and warm cinnamon rolls wafted through the air.

With Bob out, that left three on the sales floor to write work orders and assist the mob of customers. Despite being aware of the capacity issues, Mr. Calvin was hesitant to hire new employees. He knew we were always busy with inventory, especially spring, summer, and fall seasons and this year seemed busier than ever before. Yet Mr. Calvin seemed quite preoccupied. Perhaps it was just the summer heat draining his energy and patience.

The month of August wore a golden crown, basking in the warm embrace of the sun. The landscape was bathed in a languid glow, as if time itself had slowed down to soak in the last rays of summer. But with each passing day, I couldn't help but notice the gradual retreat of daylight, signaling the approaching end of the season. As if mirroring this transition, I also began to take note of the black SUV's disappearance from its usual spot on the street. No longer a distracting figure like a fly on a white piece of bread.

Time's cadence seemed to be different. Evolved. Then, unexpectedly, all sound ceased. An eerie stillness settled over my world. As if it was holding its breath, waiting for something to happen.

"It must be over. Finally, over." I whispered. A soothing tide of relief enveloped my heart as my eyes scanned the empty streets. Bentley and I encountered so much adversity and it felt as though the darkness would never lift. And yet, in the depth of our agony, resilience blossomed. Here we were, standing at a new beginning - a chance for us to start afresh. But how could I be sure that this was the right way forward? Fear of the unknown clung to each step tenaciously, at every thought of Alex and the possibility of freedom.

With a deep breath, and my head held high, I looked at the sky and winked my right eye. "Father, I know you know me best. I believe you did not bring me this far to leave me now. Show me the way." Whispering my petition, I walked to the breakroom and picked up the latest publication of the local paper. Turning to page three of the Classifieds with a red sharpie in hand, I circled some promising job openings. It was time for positive change.

"Hope!" Jerry waved to me with urgency. "Mr. Calvin wants everyone down front on the sales floor." Jerry was pushing his hand truck across the showroom swaying from side to side as if he was trying to find his balance.

"Mr. Calvin called a meeting to discuss the company's future." Amy from the cash office chimed in.

Everyone gathered in small groups, shoulder to shoulder, waiting to hear the usual pitch of motivation and sales forecasts for the next quarter. Mr. Calvin loved numbers and seemed to get a high on presentations.

"A new direction is on the horizon for us, folks. Corporate feels that Selma is not growing in the right direction and, well, our bottom line. Sadly, Walford's is on the way out! This store will close in three months, and we will start by laying off our night crew. The sales team will be next and the cash office last. I am very sorry." The room became hushed.

"Wow! Mr. Calvin, just like that, huh?" Jerry rose to his feet.

"I am sorry, Jerry."

Wow was right. None of us saw that news coming, and it hit us hard. Jerry had a new baby. Amy was a newlywed with a new mortgage. Sarah from credit just lost her husband, and two of the four salespeople transitioned to our store six months prior. Talk about timing.

We shuffled out of the meeting in a stunned daze, each of us avoiding eye contact and barely managing a nod as we passed. I quickly sized up my colleagues, observing their despairing expressions that had become all too familiar. Our futures had plunged into uncertainty; not only were jobs at stake, but our family's livelihoods would depend on the outcome.

My stomach twisted in anxious knots. Thankfully, I'd already started searching for employment before Mr. Calvin announced the store was ceasing operations. The search was now more desperate—I needed to find something fast and even sooner than expected.

The next week everyone seemed lull, and the atmosphere was depressing. Mr. Calvin was tasked with closeouts and inventory while the sales team greeted and assisted customers taking advantage of last-minute bargains.

"Hope, you have a phone call on line one." The voice echoing to me from the credit office where she'd spent the last decade was Sarah McPherson. She was always cordial and neatly dressed in her belted maxi skirts paired with fitted blouses and boyfriend blazers. With her perfectly coiffed blonde hair and impeccable attention to detail, she was such an integral part of our team.

"Thanks, Sarah." I waved to acknowledge her as I made my way across the showroom. There was still a bit of hesitancy in me as I stared at the phone.

"Hello, this Hope."

"Hope Everly?" A new and unfamiliar voice inquired.

"Yes." I confirmed, hoping it wasn't a bill collector tracking me down on my job.

"This is Monica with Our World is Changing, and we have your resume. You applied for an Executive Director's position with us, but we have another position that just came open. Are you free next Tuesday at 2:30pm?"

"Yes!" I couldn't believe it. At last, a callback.

"Great! We are located on Water Street. Are you familiar with that area?" I remembered driving past that location on my way to Walford's.

"Yes, I know exactly where you are." My mind was racing with excitement.

"Great! I look forward to meeting you."

Taken aback, I placed the receiver in its cradle and slowly raised my head. My eyes widened with gratitude. It was as if all my prayers had been answered in that single moment. I felt alive with enthusiasm. Feelings I'd forgotten. A torrent of warm and vibrant emotions surged through my body, like wildflowers blooming in a barren desert.

With a renewed sense of purpose, I glided to the warehouse. Scanning the room for an unoccupied box to store my personal belongings. Why wait until my last day to gather a few essential items? Mr. Calvin clarified we were all out of a job as soon as he sold the very last piece of furniture.

"Hope, there is a guy that has some questions about a bedframe. Can you help him?" The squealer. Just over my right shoulder holding a box of pillows.

"Sure, Jerry. Where is he?" I snapped. He still had that guilty look on his face and couldn't square me in the eye.

"He is over by the Bayhill sets near the side door." I gave Jerry an eye roll and proceeded to help the customer.

As I approached the man, I was met with a gentle, yet vulnerable chill. Everything about him, from his long dark trench coat that draped his legs below the knees, to the shine of his brown alligator shoes. Every detail seemed to trigger a familiar emotion within me. His fedora perched confidently atop his head, like Humphrey Bogart with timeless style and swagger. My heart fluttered as a warm flush filled my cheeks.

"I know this man," I whispered.

As he turned to greet me, I saw a face that I had remembered so fondly. The corners of his mouth turned up slightly, revealing the dimples I knew so very well. He was like a character from my own personal movie, and I couldn't help but feel a fervor at the sight of him. His face was that of an old friend, fondly lit up with a gentle smile that complimented his telling eyes. Eyes that spoke to me without a single word uttered from his lips.

"Can you help me, ma'am?"

"Louis Monroe!" My lips delighted at the feeling of that bouncing off my tongue.

"Hello Gorgeous!" His gaze traveled over every feature of my face, as if trying to capture and hold on to it forever.

"What has it been, like forever?" I joked.

"Not quite, but it has been too long." He smelled of fresh bergamot and cedarwood. Every whiff of his aftershave drew me in.

"What brings you into Walford's?" I let out a breath.

"I will be honest. While I was looking at these beautiful bedroom suites, I was hoping to run into you."

"Well, here I am. How can I help you?" I could have melted away.

His dreamy brown eyes were hard to look away from. He'd always been such a gorgeous man. As far back as I could remember he always captivated me. We always had that special something between us, an ember that never died out. He and I just clicked from the very first moment our eyes met. It was an instant spark. Louis was just starting out as an apprentice in the pre-need sales industry while also working his way through college. Later, I heard he opened his own public relations firm and a vast network of not-for-profit organizations. I even read about him in Forbes, just last year.

Louis, a man driven by ambition, always set his eyes on the horizon and his sights aimed at conquering the world. It was as if a spotlight had been trained on him, highlighting his sharp features and intense gaze. There was a magnetic pull that drew us towards each other, simply unexplainable. I suddenly remembered what he told me all those years ago, "I feel like I've known you my whole life." As if we were meant to be together, and nothing would ever change that. But something did.

"If you could get me some prices on these two sets and write down your phone number. I would appreciate that very much." Louis grinned, making his way over to me with confident strides. I wanted so much to give Louis my number, but I also knew that I wasn't ready to entertain the thought of moving on just yet. I also did not want to bring anyone into my broken world with all its ambiguities.

"Here you go, the figures you asked for." With my hand stretched out to meet his, I felt the hairs on my arm stand up.

"What about your phone number?" His eyes held mine for what seemed like an eternity.

"Louis, while it is so good to see you again, I am not ready for a relationship right now. I am going through some things, and it just would not be fair to bring you into it."

"Why not let me decide that?" His comeback was swift and unexpected. I responded with a kind smile.

"Trust me, right now is not a good time for me." Part of me felt regret. He nodded and reached inside his coat pocket.

"Well, here is my number. When the time is right, call me." His business card, elegant and luxurious, was the perfect representation of him. Raised lettering adorned it with a gold embossed embellishment. I couldn't help but admire it for a few moments, not wanting him to leave. Before I could say anything, he smiled and turned to walk away.

I took in every angle of him as I watched him go, unsure of what to do next. The only thing I knew was, I felt something stir inside of me when he spoke. He left me with an undeniable connection to him. Louis exuded an air of genuineness and understanding, while also maintaining an aura of mystery and distance.

As much as I was drawn to him, I knew the timing was wrong. I needed to prioritize my career and find some financial stability. Deep down I was terrified of what taking that next step with him would mean for me. I was scared to death. What if Alex resurfaced? Or the black SUV? I couldn't put Louis in the line of fire, nor could I explain the hell I'd been hiding and expect him to understand it. Maybe someday we would meet again, in a different place and time.

Fear controlled my life for so long, like having a second skin, always clinging to my body. Despite desperately wanting to believe it was all behind me, I couldn't kick the habit of constantly looking over my shoulder and doubting everyone's intentions. There was Carl's voice in my head telling me I could not live my life in constant fear, but the wounds of my past were raw. Relationships gave me intense bouts of anxiety and shattered any trust I had left.

On Tuesday morning, my stomach was a bundle of knots as I prepared for my interview. Saying a quiet prayer of thanks and affirmation, I could almost feel God's presence in the air. I steeled myself and walked into the interview with confidence. There were three people sitting behind a table for the panel interview. Each had several questions in relation to the position and each one took notes on a yellow writing pad. The brass, Monica, I recognized from the phone call. Her voice seemed enthusiastic and polite.

"Hope, we have an Assistant Director's role that we need to fill. It could be a perfect fit for you with your experience and capabilities. The job would be an excellent starting point for you in the non-profit sector and the initial salary is set at $52,000 a year."

My eyes widened in astonishment at the generous figure. $52K, a sum of money that seemed unimaginable and far beyond my previous experience. My heart thrummed as I considered the latitude of the opportunity. It was like a door opening to a brand-new world.

My hands trembled with anticipation as I felt thrilled and overwhelmed all at once. The interviewer continued to explain the benefits and perks that came with the position: health insurance, paid time off, extended leave, and professional development. It seemed like a dream job. The questions were numerous, and it felt like I'd been in the interview for days.

After two hours, I finally stood and exited the room. I shuffled out into the lobby with my head spinning. Replaying their questions over and over in my mind – had I given the correct answers? The interview had been nerve-wracking, but I was certain that I had at least made a memorable impression.

Walking out of the building, looking up at the sky, I took a deep breath in. Suddenly, I felt the weight of all my worries and anxieties lift off my shoulders. I knew there was still a chance that I wouldn't get the job, but for the first time in months, I felt determined to take control of my life in a way that I hadn't since Carl's passing. I stepped out of my fears and into the unknown, and in that very moment, somehow, it was enough.

The weeks seemed to drag on as I waited in anticipation for an answer. Waiting was hard, and the days were filled with nervous energy. My thoughts raced as I wondered what I could have done differently during the interview - how I could have convinced the panel that I was the best candidate for the role. I had spent countless hours rehearsing my answers, studying the company's history, and perfecting my body language. But was it enough?

"Are you nervous, dear?" Mom noticed my pacing back and forth.

"I am somewhat anxious." I answered her with a smile. What was taking so long? Maybe they selected someone else. So many thoughts raging and intensifying my anxiety. At last, the phone rang. I paused before answering, the significance of the moment spiking my adrenaline. With bated breath, I prepared myself for the outcome but couldn't answer the call. I just stood there. Mom reacted.

"Hello? Yes. One moment." Mom winked at me to indicate it was ok. I walked over to her. My voice shaking, clearing my throat trying to inject confidence into my voice.

"Hello. This is Hope."

"Congratulations! You have been chosen as our next Assistant Director!" Monica's words hung in the air, completely suspended, as I tried to absorb her announcement. Tears of relief flooded my face.

"Thank you so much, Monica! I cannot wait to start. I would like to give two weeks' notice to my current employer if that is permissible?" My way of being professional.

"Certainly, as expected. We will see you in two weeks from today, Monday at 9am."

A two-week notice to an employer going out of business was unnecessary, but I felt it was still the right thing to do.

From that defining moment, a newfound sense of self-worth coursed through my veins. It was as if a dormant power had been awakened, with frontiers stretched out before me like an endless horizon. And like a butterfly on fire, ablaze with an illuminated energy, Hope Everly had a career. This was a fresh start, and she was going to *live*.

Celebrations began with my family. My eyes could hardly hold back the tears as I shared the news with mom and Bentley. Mom, always the emotional one, let out a loud gasp of delight, her eyes welling up with tears that she tried to hide behind her hands.

"What wonderful news, love!" she exclaimed, pulling me into a tight embrace. Bentley, who was usually reserved, was now bouncing around the living room like a wild animal.

"This is just the beginning! We are making some changes." I assured Bentley. "Soon, we will have our very own place and you will have your own room."

"You mean it, ma?" His eyes filled with anticipation.

"Absolutely!"

"Will it be ok for us to leave granny and be on our own?" He inquired with a touch of concern. Placing a gentle hand on his shoulder, brushing a small curly lock from his eyes, I answered

"Yes, baby. It is time we stop living our lives in fear."

"So, is it okay for us to go places now? Other than school and work, I mean." Bentley's eyes sparkled.

"Baby, we have lived in hiding far too long. We must make a life for ourselves and ask Jehovah to be our shield."

It was a declaration of freedom, a courageous leap out of the shadows and stepping boldly into the light -- like a blazing phoenix rising from the ashes.

Fear shall not break me, although I tire.

For courage blooms an eternal fire.

Up from the ashes I take flight-

My wings aflame, of a resplendent light.

Chapter Twelve

B entley was sprouting. His once lanky frame was now filled out with lean muscle and his posture was straight and confident. His curls framing his face perfectly and his smile was big and bright, making his handsome features even more prominent. His turquoise glasses added a pop of color to his overall scholarly appearance.

A passionate reader, Bentley devoured books from many genres, and was always eager to discuss what he'd read with anyone who would listen. From classic literature to philosophy to the latest scientific discoveries. His attachment to books was evident in the way he would lose himself in their pages. His face contorting with emotion and his eyes darting across the words as if they were alive. His fingers would trace the sentences, almost as if he were trying to absorb every ounce of meaning from the paper. And when he would finish a book, he would close it slowly, savoring the last moments before placing it back on the shelf with reverence.

But despite his love for literature, his true passion was art. His sketches were a reflection of his inner turmoil and his deepest desires. Each stroke of his pencil was purposeful, each line intricately placed to convey a feeling or an idea. He poured his heart and soul into his drawings, using them as an outlet for all the emotions he couldn't express through words, drawing portraits of people and sketching from memory the characters he read about in his books.

"I can see that the scholarship money is helping out," I remarked fondly to Bentley as I watched his pencil effortlessly glide across the paper.

"Creating something from my own thoughts or ideas feels so rewarding. It's how I know that I want to be an artist someday—to make a difference with my work. Art gives me a sense of freedom. It makes me feel alive." His eyes sparkled as he spoke.

I smiled at him proudly, knowing that Bentley was furthering himself in ways that no one else could understand. He was carving a path for himself with something that gave him fulfillment beyond anything else in life. My heart swelled as I watched him pursue his passion with such enthusiasm. One day Bentley would be well renowned for his talents. I was sure of it.

Filled with vibrant colors, his drawings came alive with each stroke of the pencil, adding depth and vitality to the images. The lines were precise and intentional, showcasing his unique skill. Images depicting figures in a powerful stance, as if to symbolize a new position and the desire to prove oneself, reminding me of my new responsibilities as an executive.

"*Assistant Executive Director, Hope Everly.*" I spoke softly into existence, a proclamation of my new identity. The words hung in the air like a gossamer veil, gently caressing the atmosphere and swathing me in a sense of pride and purpose. "I am no longer who I once was," I said, my voice barely above a whisper. While the road ahead was still uncertain, I was ready to embrace it.

The morning sun was blinding to the west, transforming the rural landscape into a breathtaking tapestry. Over the Arch of Freedom and into the city, still cloaked in the remnants of dawn, life was awakening to the day's rhythm. 315 Water Street wasn't difficult to locate. One thing I loved most about living in a small town, it was easy to navigate.

Towering above older buildings nearby, the Monroe Building was a newly restored location with modern flair combined with architectural history, beautifully redesigned, and situated in the heart of downtown. Inside, was Our World Is Changing. A prestigious organization dedicated to creating a better future for underserved communities.

I never expected to experience such a powerful sense of purpose and belonging, but as soon as I stepped into the building, it felt like home. The high-ceilings and well-lit rooms were flooded with natural light that illuminated the shelves of books, the vibrant artworks, and the inviting solid oak desk in the middle of the foyer. Marbled floors covered the entry and lobby area with a shine almost blinding.

"You must be Hope Everly?" A neatly dressed brunette met me with an inviting smile.

"Yes, I am Ms. Everly." Her perfume was a clean brisk scent that was almost overwhelming.

"I will show you to your office."

The hallway was long and wide, but we soon arrived at an immaculate space. In a bold black ink on a crisp, white business card, a name to go with the title. *Hope Everly* stood out in elegant cursive script. The title, *Assistant Executive Director*, gleamed proudly on the gold nameplate that adorned my cherry wood desk, catching the light and reflecting it onto the walls. The office was sophisticated and modern, with glass walls showcasing the bustling city outside.

The air had a faint scent of fresh coffee and a hint of florals, likely from the arrangement of roses and pincushion flowers on my desk. This was a place of refuge and possibility, where ideas could come alive, and creativity could thrive. I was ready to feel alive.

In a matter of weeks, it seemed I'd gone from the corner office to my own corner of the world. I was so proud of my accomplishments. But my newfound sense of pride was tempered with a heightened sense of responsibility. This was a place of action, and I was resolute in my commitment to help make the world a better place.

Through conversations with colleagues and members of the organization, I quickly came to understand the scope of the challenge: to create a just and equitable society. Tasked with creating relevant solutions that would reduce inequality and increase opportunities for all. My days seemed to blur together as I collaborated with revolutionaries, exploring innovative ideas that could help shape our future for the better.

As we put together our plan for action, it was clear we had big dreams for transforming our world into one based on equity, and inclusion– and we refused to give up until we achieved the mission. My work gave me a broader understanding of philanthropy and how it could be both practical and powerful.

My work at Our World Is Changing didn't just help others; it transformed me as well. By giving back to those in need and striving towards greater social justice, I could find meaning in my life—allowing me to discover my identity as well as what truly mattered most among humanity. Knowing firsthand all about inequality and injustice from my own life experiences, I could now see how others were affected by it too. I believed God opened this door for me to make a difference in my community. A door opened to reveal to me the hardest part was simply taking the first steps–and once I did, I discovered that anything is possible.

While we shared the Monroe building with two other businesses, it was the second floor where most of the action happened. Located in that area, this unique space had all the makings of an innovative hub for creative connection and collaboration.

Directly next to the Monroe building was a newly constructed parking garage, which always gave me the creeps. While it was well-maintained, it never felt inviting; the dim lighting and lack of activity made it seem somewhat spooky. I was often reminded of its presence during our outdoor events in the summer, when its towering structure provided an ominous backdrop for us to work against. Despite its rather forbidding aesthetic, this space served an essential mission; it allowed guests and participants to park without having to venture too far from the building and it accommodated the elderly with greater access away from the street.

As Assistant Director, I was tasked with overseeing and organizing our events. A welcomed distraction from the strange, burning feeling in my gut that had been gnawing away at me for weeks, unyielding. No matter how hard I tried to push it away, the feeling would remain–a constant reminder of something I couldn't quite pinpoint, disturbing my newfound peace. Perhaps I was just nervous about our upcoming annual conference, especially since I was the Chair this year. I was feeling the pressure of my responsibilities, but I would not allow it to defeat me.

Then one evening, just days before the conference would take place, I had another eerie encounter with that gut feeling that I could not dislodge. I sat alone in my room, eyes glued to the bedroom window as I watched the rain pour down. Consumed by a lingering, restless feeling, I found it daunting to meditate on my thoughts when mom came in with the mail.

"Looks like bills and junk mail, Hope." The stack was mixed with colorful circulars and white envelopes. "Oh wait. Here is a letter that came for you with no return address." Mom peeped at the envelope before handing it over.

"That is odd. Probably a piece of junk mail, most likely a sales flyer."

A plain white envelope with a smudge stain across the back near the seal that smelled of pine bark and lavender. Yet when I opened it, I found something much more interesting inside. A small invitation card requesting my attendance at an event to be held at Jemison's Theater Hall, next to the parking garage, adjacent to the Monroe building.

The invitation made no mention of why the requestor was hosting this event or who the intended audience was, only indicating that there would be something special awaiting me there. The event was dated for two months from today's date. I assumed the agenda to correspond with philanthropy.

"Must be a donor giving a soiree or something."

"Sounds like fun, dear," mom chimed. "Two months from today, you said?" Her expression matched the curious glint in her eyes.

"Yes, mom. Why?"

"Isn't that Bentley's art fair and exhibit night?" She held my gaze for a brief moment.

"Oh, gosh! You are so right. Well, maybe I can still work it out and just pop into the event after Bentley's art fair."

She nodded in agreement and concluded, "that sounds viable." Still, I wondered why there was no return address. Odd. I was sure it was an oversight of someone in charge of mailers. Human error. The sender did say there was something special to be held and I could hardly wait to attend. But as the day of the annual conference dawned, my stomach was a tangled knot of anxiety and apprehension, threatening to unravel at any moment.

There were at least five hundred people in attendance and at least one hundred vendors vying for their attention. The cacophony of voices and the clatter of coins from the beverage carts mixed with the heady scent of freshly brewed coffee delighted my nose.

Scanning the crowd, I recognized some familiar faces and noted the tension in their expressions. I could feel the collective energy in the room, like a palpable force pulsing through the air as if everyone was awaiting something important.

"Hope! I didn't know that you would be here. Who invited you?" Before I could answer, Monica proceeded, "Never mind. I am glad you came. You can go on stage and present your program."

Talk about on the spot! What just happened here? I was so unprepared. The enormity of the event was quite daunting. My palms became sweaty with nervous energy and my heart hammered inside my chest. Knowing that I had to go on stage and deliver a presentation in front of this vast crowd made me dizzy. I took a deep breath and thought about what I would say. As if sensing my hesitation, one of the organizers came over and held up two fingers.

"It's go time, Hope! You are up in two." He offered to walk with me to the stage, but I waved him off.

Stepping up to the podium, a trickle of sweat rolled off my forehead as the crowd hushed. The lump in my throat made it hard to swallow and I could feel my knees wobble. Waving from the far left of the stage was Monica, giving me a smile of encouragement. It was a small gentle gesture, but it meant everything to me. It was a moment to savor, and not to fear.

Standing on that stage, about to speak to a room full of people, the hot lights were blinding to my eyes. Although distracting, I reminded myself of those who were genuinely interested in what I had to say. Shoulders back, I smiled and looked out at the audience–a sea of faces staring back at me expectantly–and began my delivery.

My words flowed effortlessly as I spoke about the mission of the organization and shared snippets of successes and failures I'd encountered in my tenure there. A few nods and smiles from the crowd assured me of their attention. As I finished, thunderous applause reverberated through the walls of the room. It was a surreal feeling to know that I had not only overcome my own fears but also connected with such an influential crowd so significantly.

Walking off stage, my eyes caught sight of a small figure hiding in the shadows at the edge of the crowd. I squinted and tried to make out the face, but the bright stage lights made it impossible to see. People were darting everywhere as I kept searching for the figure that had caught my attention.

Losing sight of the inconspicuous silhouette among the crowd and vendor booths, I felt there was something familiar about the figure, but its recognition eluded my mind. I shook my head and pushed my way through the dense crowd.

Out of the corner of my eye, I saw someone quickly passing by and then disappearing through the exit doors. Instinctively, I followed behind them, closing the distance between us as we neared the parking garage entrance. The shadow vanished as the door closed shut before I could catch it and locked from the outside. Baffled, I struggled to recall where I had encountered that figure before. My thoughts became muddled, and I couldn't seem to grasp onto any specific memory. Why did this bother me so much?

Throughout the night I felt like I was being followed or watched, but I saw no one that looked suspicious. I shrugged off my unease and eventually forgot about it as the rest of the night went by in a blur of presentations and conversations with vendors.

"Hope, great job tonight!" Monica exclaimed.

"Thanks. I appreciate that!" Her praise took me by surprise. Before she could dart away, she turned and reached inside her pocket.

"Hey, I almost forgot. Someone left this cute little note for you." Monica placed the decorative note card into my hand.

"Who gave you this?" I inquired. But before she could answer, a donor took her by the arm and drew her away. I put the notecard inside my pocket and collected my belongings.

After locking up, I made my way down the stairwell and into the garage. The night air was cool and still, a stark contrast to the warmth of the crowded building that lingered in my bones. I paused for a moment at the bottom of the stairs, feeling a pang of apprehension, recalling the mysterious figure in the audience. I knew it had to be just nerves and paranoia, so I continued on my way.

"Get a grip, Hope!" I found myself whispering.

The city was dark and quiet, as if it were secretly in waiting of something to come. I could feel a strange energy in the air, a palpable throb, like an animal ready to pounce. My senses were on high alert, the hairs on the back of my neck standing at attention. I walked faster. An unseen presence seemed to walk along with me, like a presence that I could sense but couldn't quite see. There was an eerie tingle flirting with my senses, although I saw no one. It was like a strange pull—to where I did not know—but I couldn't deny it either.

My feet moved of their own accord, carrying me along in a great wave, a current of electrified spook, ominous and powerful. Shadows seemed to dance around the edges of my vision, and now and then I glimpsed a figure that wasn't there, just at the corner of my eye. Every step I took seemed to echo, as if someone was walking right behind me. I could hear the faint sound of breathing, heavy and labored, but still no visible presence.

Finally, I reached the gate that opened to the street access. I stepped through, and the wave of fear faded away, as if it had never existed. I looked back, but saw no trace of the mysterious figure. Desperate to reach and settle inside the safety of my car, I secured my purse and jacket on the passenger seat and locked the doors.

Reaching into my jacket pocket, I pulled out the note that Monica gave to me earlier. The textured envelope was a pastel blue color with a wax seal on the back flap. There was no indication of whom it was from, but the handwriting on the front of it seemed shadowy, forceful.

With trembling hands, I carefully opened the envelope, revealing a crisp, yellowed piece of card stock paper.

Carefully unfolding, I read the words written within it: "*I enjoyed your nervy little presentation, and I am inspired by your courage. You will need that bravery once more, much sooner than you think.*" An eeriness enveloped me as the thoughts of this person watching me on stage throughout the night played fiddle with my nerves.

The words hung heavy in the air as my stomach clenched in panic. The sounds of an occasional car passing by on the street outside, drew my attention. Its headlights cutting through the darkness. I carefully tucked the paper back into its envelope and shoved it away into my pocket. "It is nothing," I assured myself.

On the drive home, my thoughts were cluttered, rambling with the sequence of the night—a strange figure at the conference, shadows in the garage, and the mysterious note with a cryptic message. Clouded with fear as I pulled into the driveway, I just knew that somehow, despite all the mystifying strangeness, it seemed like everything was starting to connect—but how? I needed to think.

Once inside, the house smelled of hot apple pie and the air was warm and soothing, like a fleece blanket on a cool night. Bentley settled in his usual spot in the living room, surrounded by countless pieces of paper and a stack of colored pencils, along with his artwork. I marveled at his drawings, each one pinpointing a moment in time, meticulously dated and numbered, each one telling a story of their own. His talent was mesmerizing.

"Did you have a good time tonight, dear?"

I hesitated before answering, not wanting to reveal the swirl of emotions inside me.

"Umm…. yes, mom. It was… an interesting night."
Answering nonchalantly, I couldn't quite put into words
the mixture of emotions I was feeling. The night had been
one to remember.

After saying goodnight to Bentley, I lit some candles
and ran a hot bath. I took a deep breath before stepping
into it, letting the steam fill my lungs. My thoughts, still
whirling from the evening, were wild and restless. Still
so many unanswered questions. Who sent the note? Who
was the figure in the crowd? Was someone following me?
Was I just paranoid?

As I relaxed into the bath, I began to pray. I petitioned
for cover and protection from whatever was chasing me.
To unveil the evil that lurked in this town so it could be
brought to justice. I thought about the black SUV, Alex,
Carl's murder, and the silent caller, wondering how the
pieces fit together.

The warmth of the water lulled me into a peaceful
state, and soon I had drifted off into a deep sleep. All too
quickly, it seemed, I awoke to find myself still submerged
in the bath with most of its warmth gone. I dried off
and changed into my pajamas before retreating to my
bedroom.

Lying down in bed, exhaustion tugged at me and
soon enough, my racing thoughts faded away as sleep
embraced me.

Bang, Bang, Bang, Bang, Bang, Bang! I jumped up in the
middle of the bed, my heart racing, and my skin damp
with sweat. My heart raced wildly, my breath became
short, the tightness in my chest made it hard to breathe
as sheer panic tortured me. All too insistent, a hollow
familiarity set in, soon realizing it was just a nightmare.
Out of nowhere, that memory was haunting me again.
Why now? I tried so hard to push it out of my mind, but

there it was, back again with a vengeance. Knowing I was up for the night, I switched on the lamp next to the clock at 4:00 a.m. I stepped into my fuzzy house slippers and headed for the kitchen. Time to make coffee and get on with the day.

Unable to calm the unsettling emotions from the previous night, I hastily donned my navy pinstripe suit, straightened my hair, and grabbed my black leather tote. The weight of it on my arm, a familiar comfort, reminded me of all the important briefs and contracts it had carried. But today, its usual purpose felt insignificant.

The morning sun poked through the concrete towers of the parking garage, casting an unforgiving glare on my face. I took a deep breath and plastered a forced smile across my mouth before stepping into the elevator. The feeling that this day would be different was clinging onto me. And when I reached the lobby, my gut feeling proved to be true. The receptionist leaned in and whispered to me.

"Hope, the CEO of GenFive is waiting for you in your office." Her eyes mirrored the same shock I felt trying to digest her words.

After a brief pause, I straightened my posture and gave her a wink. My stilettos clicked against the polished marble flooring as I made my way down the hallway towards my office.

"Good morning, Mr. Prince. So good to see you again."

Mr. Prince nodded; his usually gruff demeanor softened by the pleasantness of the morning. He sat with his Panama hat resting on his knee.

"Hope, I will be brief. I have an eleven-fifteen flight to Chicago that I have to catch." Now erect in his chair, his dark brown eyes met mine. His face was angular and chiseled, with strong cheekbones and a command-ing jawline. "I was incredibly impressed with you last night. You spoke eloquently and your passion for your work here at Our World Is Changing is impressive. As you know, GenFive is one of the largest non-profits in the world, headquartered in Chicago. We manage over twelve trillion dollars in assets."

My cheeks flushed with pride. Nodding, my face a portrait of seriousness, I worked up a quick reply.

"Yes, sir. I am moved by the company's presence and mission and I do admire your work." I leaned backwards into my chair.

Mr. Prince paused for a moment, gauging my reac-tion, then he continued. "We want you to direct our next major expansion." He grinned; an almost clever smile painted his lips. I could not believe his offer. What did he just say? I stared at him, dumbstruck. This was a once-in-a-lifetime opportunity, one that might catapult my career.

"We need someone with your experience and leader-ship ability to take us to the next level."

"Mr. Prince, I don't know what to say. I am deeply honored and humbled that you would even consider me for the position." As attractive as the offer was, I had to make sure I fully understood the parameters before accepting.

"Mr. Prince," I began. "Would this require reloca-tion?" I noted his smile, seeming to understand my hes-itation.

"It's negotiable, for a while, with frequent travel to Chicago, but we are looking to expand and would like you to oversee our operations in the Southeast. You could potentially remain in the region, but you will need to start in eight months."

"I see." My brow furrowed. My hand fidgeted with the pen atop my desk while I studied the idea.

"Hope, not only the opportunity, but the compensation would make what you earn here look like pocket change. We are talking six figures. Just think about it and let me know what you decide."

As Mr. Prince walked away, my mind raced with the myriads of developments this could unfold for me. However, uprooting my life and moving was an intimidating thought. It would mean leaving the oversight of family and friends for the unknown, and that concerned me. Was timing right for this move?

I spent all day mulling over the offer from GenFive. This was my third year at Our World Is Changing and I was perfectly happy as Assistant Director, but this offer was too good to pass up. What I could accomplish with six figures in the bank was mind blowing. It was an offer that danced about, inviting with one hand, and yet firmly holding onto its own terms with the other. A tempting balance of opportunity and practicality, with a hint of adventure. A temptress, toying with my emotions, alluring and irresistible, until an old nemesis appeared. Fear.

Traveling to Chicago and within the Southeast would require organizing care for Bentley and being away for extended periods of time. My life was already in such disarray and perplexity. Although, eight months wasn't exactly tomorrow, there was still so much to consider. Was this even doable?

Reeling from the morning's visit with Mr. Prince, I was distracted as I walked across the cold grey concrete in the parking garage. The echoes of my footsteps resonated against the hard surface, creating a rhythmic cadence that reverberated throughout the cavernous space. I could feel eyes on me, like I was being watched, as if an invisible gaze had woven a web around me. Instinctively, I turned around, anticipating someone following closely behind. But, just as before, there was no one there. I shivered and continued walking, only this time at a faster pace. Click, click, click, the click of my heels grew louder. I could swear I heard footsteps coming from behind me, quickening their pace to match mine.

Once I reached my car, I discovered a yellow envelope carefully positioned under the left windshield wiper. Snatching it up promptly, I entered my car, meticulously ensuring the doors were securely locked. My tires squealed against the surface, rounding each corner with urgency before exiting the garage.

Merely two blocks awaited the city's lone coffee shop, a haven that beckoned with the promise of a brief respite. My heart thumping loudly, I opened the envelope. There was no signature, no return address, no phone number, and devoid of the sender's name. The message was scrawled in black ink; the words menacing and dangerous, as I read: "*Your time has come, and you have something that I want. You can't hide. I will collect it .... soon.*"

Staring at the crumpled yellow paper in my hand, I took note of the jagged scrawled letters, slanted and angry. Each character seemed to bear the imprint of an unbridled and forceful rage. The situation was getting out of control. How could I involve law enforcement and do it quietly? I knew of only one person I could call.

Chapter Thirteen

Detective Thomas. I had his business card in my wallet. I reached for my phone and dialed the number. "Hello? This is Hope Everly. I need to speak with you as soon as possible. It is urgent." Leaving a voicemail was not ideal, but since he did not answer, what else could I do? He was my best bet for privacy, and he already knew my backstory. I was clearly in over my head with this one, and I needed help.

This had to be someone who was obsessed with me. Someone who would stop at nothing to get my attention. I shuddered at the thought, but I had a sinking feeling that it was Alex. After all this time, was he back to torment me even more? The more I searched for the answer, the more I felt like I was losing my mind. Why now? Why come back for me now? I sat in the coffee shop's parking lot for at least twenty minutes before heading for home. The drive would give me time to process and think about the mess I was in.

About halfway home, the headlights of a car suddenly appeared in my rearview mirror. But I kept my eyes on the road ahead. I kept trying to ignore the creeping sense of unease that gnawed at me. The car stayed behind me, its headlights casting a bright glare in my mirrors. I couldn't make out the driver, but they were keeping a close pace with me around every curve along the winding road. I tried to reject the feeling that I was being followed, but the car never seemed to lose interest in the chase.

Then, as quickly as the car appeared behind me, it disappeared out of sight. I let out a sigh of relief, my heart still pounding in my chest. My foot slammed onto the gas pedal, and the engine roared as I pushed my car to its limits. The night was falling fast.

The last mile stretched out before me and once over the Budgie Creek Bridge I was home free. Adrenaline rushed with a fury of bearish energy. Rounding the corner and down the hill, sitting crossways of the bridge, there was the black SUV. The one always parked outside of Walford's. The one that disappeared and was never seen again, until now. I cringed as I slammed on the brakes.

Tires screeching to a halt as smoke rose from the rubber madly gripping the road. My heart thundered in a sudden stab of terror. The pounding rhythm matched the quickening pace of my breath. My knuckles turned white as I gripped the leather steering wheel with all my strength. The sinister black SUV loomed before me like a massive beast poised to strike. It sat there, unmoving, like a predator waiting for its prey.

With no sign of movement coming from either vehicle, I quickly put my car in reverse. The SUV driver's side door opened, but no one appeared from the darkness. Just as quickly, the door closed, and the black SUV sped away in the opposite direction. With blacked-out windows and no visible tag, there was no way to determine who was driving. With the Budgie Creek Bridge now clear, I hastened my pace. I raced home and locked all the doors.

As I entered the house, I could hear the faint sound of the TV droning in the den. Relieved that mom and Bentley were occupied and wouldn't see me, I swiftly made my way to the study. I needed a moment to gather my thoughts, to calm the tumultuous emotions that erupted within me. They couldn't see just how much I was struggling. Not Mom, with her kind but worried eyes, and certainly not Bentley, who looked up to me with nothing but admiration and trust. I had to be strong for them, to shield them from the darkness that threatened to consume me.

Sitting at my desk the next morning, I convinced myself that this had to stop. I had to find out who was stalking me and why, and before I could accept Mr. Prince's generous offer. There had to be a way out. My computer screen illuminated with multiple tabs open, each filled with research on stalking and ways to protect myself.

The wall clock continuously ticked, marking the passage of time, serving as a constant reminder that the seconds were slipping away. The bright morning light filtering in through the window illuminated my cluttered desk. Papers and files were strewn about, evidence of my frantic search for answers. Suddenly, there was a knock at the door. I looked up, momentarily startled.

UPI delivery showed up on time as usual, picking up the Director's returns to QNC shopping network and all the organization's weekly shipping. The driver always had a stack of boxes on his hand truck and always unloaded the deliveries near the stock room doors.

"Today I have a package for Hope Everly." The muscular frame with sandy blonde hair wore a deep bronze tan and spoke with a rich, smooth tone. I let out a deep sigh, grateful for the interruption. His sea blue eyes were like a cool ocean pool, ready to swim or drown in.

"Uhh, ma'am?" Waving his hand to get my attention.

"Umm, Hope Everly, you say?" Pretending not to have heard him.

"Yes, ma'am." His response was quick and affirmed.

"Ok, that would be me." Giving a nod, I reached for the package. He handed me the small computer to sign my name in acceptance.

Thinking the driver would place the brown box into my hands, he instead, placed it on the edge of my desk. Appearing hesitant; his movements hurried. My eyes scrutinized the box, quite suspiciously. It was unusual for me to receive packages at the office.

Carefully inspecting it from top to bottom, I noticed that there was no return address on the front. With a deep breath and sorted mumbling, I reached to cut open the lid. Hands shaking, I had a bad feeling about this. Frustrated, I slowly opened the box, filled with loose cuts of paper and blue confetti. The texture varied, some pieces smooth to the touch. While others possessed a slight crinkle, emitting a disconcerting rustle.

Finally, I reached the bottom of the box and uncovered a small photograph. My heart sank as I recognized the image, standing on stage, at the annual conference. But that wasn't all. Across my face was a large red X and the words: *Your time has come!* Written in red scrawled, jagged letters, slanted and angry, just like the letter.

Without thinking, I dropped the photograph onto the floor and stumbled backwards, struggling to catch my breath. As if the very essence of that moment had transformed into a haunting specter. The photo's glossy surface now reflected not just the lights of the stage but an unnerving distortion of the reality it once portrayed.

"Hey, Hope, do you have this week's calendar all filled up because I---my God! Are you okay? You look like you've seen a ghost!"

Startled by the Director, my eyes met hers in a quiver, and before she could see the photo, I concealed it with my shoe.

"Yes, I have some openings on the calendar, if needed." Quickly composing my emotions, regaining control of my demeanor. I sat down at my desk, opening my planner to the current month.

"Hope, you are always so organized. I wish everyone on my staff was more like you. You are always so put together."

The Director's words of commendation did nothing to calm my tumultuous undercurrent. I took a deep breath in and slowly released it, careful not to give away my secret.

As the Director continued to discuss her plans for the upcoming week, I began brainstorming my mystifing dilemma. Maybe I could take a leave of absence to escape from the stalker. That would give the detective a chance to listen to my voicemail and call me back. Where was he? Maybe he'd forgotten all about me.

Giving a nod here and there to acknowledge Monica's conversation, I thought, opting for a leave from work felt like a dubious choice. Especially given the timing of Mr. Prince's recent proposition. No. Somehow, I knew this had to end. "Hope, be sure to add all those items I discussed to the calendar and email me a briefing in the morning."

When Monica exited my office, I hid the photograph inside my desk under a stack of letterhead. I then took the empty box to the storeroom after cleaning up the confetti. At that point, I just wanted to go home and hide. Instead, I found my escape in a cup of caramel macchiato from the break room. The swirls inside the cup reminded me of the last time I saw those swirls, chaotic and unpredictable. I dared not entertain those thoughts. The Director popped in with a box of donuts, giving her staff the daily dose of sugar and white flour before our board meeting at 3pm.

The room was buzzing with energy as the entire team was present and ready to discuss the agenda for the upcoming week. I had only taken a few bites of my donut when I heard a knock on the door and saw the deliveryman standing in the doorway. He was holding another package. My eyes wide and fixated on the box as the Director stood to accept it and signed for it. I could feel the sweat bead up on my forehead as I watched her open the box. She eagerly dove right into the contents as I sat on the edge of my seat.

"Oh good! I have been waiting for this for months," she said. I let out a deep breath of relief as she sorted through the contents with an excited expression on her face. Having relished the moment, she disclosed a gift from a valued client—brimming with cutting-edge technology to enhance our daily operations. The revelation elevated everyone's mood, steering our focus back to the board meeting discussion.

As the topic drifted away from me, I stepped out of the room and walked back to my desk. I was still rattled and now a bit queasy. My body began to quiver as if it were trying to unshackle from something unknown. My hands twitched and spasmed, my fingers like little birds fluttering their wings in a desperate attempt to fly. I wanted to get up and move away, to run and hide from this unwelcomed feeling. But I felt paralyzed. My feet rooted to the floor.

Lost in my thoughts, suddenly I heard a voice floating in the air.

"What are you thinking about?" In all his beauty and strikingly chiseled features, dreamy brown eyes, and tailored pinstriped suit stood Louis Monroe. Overtaken by the suddenness of his presence, I was deafened to comprehend what was happening. He just stood there in a captivating vision. His smile possessed an enchanting quality that stirred my heart into a flutter. Mesmerized by his presence, I sat in silent admiration, ensconced in his confident stature. With gentleness, he repeated his question.

"What are you thinking about?" His voice carried warmth and promise. Somehow creating an atmosphere of trust where it seemed safe to share my innermost thoughts. But I couldn't bring myself to do that. Having encountered others in my past who judged me based on my life's story, I reluctantly withheld that vulnerable part of myself.

"How did you know where to find me?" Our eyes locked, while I awaited his answer. Louis smiled, a glint of mischief in his eyes.

"You are not hard to find. You are in the papers, on TV, and we are in a small town."

I felt my cheeks flush with embarrassment as I realized he had been keeping tabs on me. Was his visit a coincidence, or had he been planning this encounter all along?

"I haven't seen you since that day at Walford's, Louis."

He dropped his coat across a chair, sat on the edge of my desk, and paused for a moment before continuing.

"I wanted to see if you'd changed your mind?" His hand found mine and gently squeezed. I found myself holding my breath in anticipation of what he was going to say next. My heart raced as I waited for him to elaborate on his question, but he simply stared expectantly at me.

"Changed my mind?" Curiously shaking my head.

"Yes, about giving me your number and maybe dinner." His eyes sparkled against the interior lighting. I had to look away from his splendor and gather my focus.

"Louis, if only you knew why I hesitated in my decision. I really do need more time." I stood and moved away but I sensed his body coming closer.

"Hope, Selma is a small town. I hear things. Things that make me nervous for you but not nervous enough to give up on you."

I tried to think of a response. I could feel Louis's gaze locked onto me, intense and unwavering. I let out a deep breath as silence filled the room.

"I know more than you think I do, Hope." His words struck a chord within me, and tears welled in my eyes. He reached out and whisked away a tear from my cheek with his thumb. "So, let's get dinner - it'll be our way of saying we're both here for each other through whatever's going on." His gentleness was overpowering.

"Please, just give me some time. You are the last person I would ever want to hurt and right now—"

"Shhhhh." He shook his head, and placed his finger onto my lips. "See, there you go. Making decisions for both of us."

I felt my walls of protection begin to crumble. Despite the sadness in the room, I felt a smile take shape. Louis wrapped his arm gently around my shoulders, pulling me closer into an embrace. If only I could have melted into him and remained there in his comforting embrace.

"I am sorry, but I can't do this right now. I can't be vulnerable when I am forced to be strong."

"Hope --"

"No, please." I took his hand. "I appreciate you stopping by, and it is always so delightful to see you. I need to get on home to Bentley. Please, try to understand."

"I understand." Louis gave a nod. I could tell he was trying his best not to press me.

"It will be here when you're ready." He winked and squeezed my hand.

Louis had a way of taking me to another time and place without ever leaving the room. I knew that he meant every word that flowed from his lips. We said our goodbyes, and then Louis made his way down the corridor to the lobby. I watched him go with a heavy heart and a lump in my throat, while also relieved by his patience.

In the quiet moments after Louis departed, I examined my feelings for him and reflected on what always happens between us. That moment that stands still in time. That moment when nothing else matters but our feverish chemistry. A magnetic attraction that defies all reasoning. Right before the dreaded fear sets in.

The prospect of vulnerability terrified me more than anything, making it impossible for Louis to become a part of my hazardous life. Although, ready for my nightmare to end, what concerned me the most was how would it end?

The close of the day always gave me anxiety, and the parking garage gave me chills. I never knew when or where or what would be hiding, waiting for me. From the breezeway to my car, I got a sinking feeling in the pit of my stomach. My eyes anxiously combed the windshield, searching for the ominous note that I dreaded might manifest. At each hint of irregularity, I froze, as a shiver of alarm overcame me. But today, there was no note.

As my pace quickened, drawing closer to my car, I heard a noise coming from behind a nearby column. All the hairs on my head stood on end as I felt an icy chill rush up my spine. Taking a deep breath, my attention diverted to the noise. I quickly walked backwards to my car. Swirling around in a panic as tires squalled from a utility van rounding the corner, fleeting past me.

Without hesitation, I jumped into my car and locked the doors. The windows fogged from my heavy breathing. Fear was dripping off me like sweat. Holding my breath, I listened for any sign of movement around me, but all was dead quiet.

Igniting the engine, my intent was escaping as quickly as possible. I navigated through the maze of parking levels, accidently engaging my wipers. The mist sliding down my windshield closely resembled my tears, tracing the contours of my essence. I could feel the seat of my car beneath me, the worn leather cupping me like being wrapped in a blanket of comfort. I could feel the heated steering wheel and the blood pulsing through my veins as Louis's words echoed in my mind. Why couldn't we have met at a different time and place in our lives? If he knew about Alex, he'd run fast and as far away from me as possible. I was sure of it.

The powerful roar of the engine vibrated in my ears. The screech of the tires melded with the asphalt as I slammed into my breaks, pausing in the driveway. From the side porch, the harmonizing sound of laughter could be heard coming from the living room. It was the time of day when Mom and Bentley were sitting on the couch, eyes glued to their favorite game show.

Entering the house, the mouth-watering aroma of freshly baked bread filled the air, making my stomach grumble with hunger. I greeted them both with a weak smile, pretending as if I wasn't rattled to the core. Forcing myself to laugh along with them, while my mind retrieved thoughts of Alex and Louis, Monica, and Mr. Prince. Mom patted the seat next to her on the couch and I obediently obliged, sinking into the soft cushions.

We watched in a peaceful silence until the credits started rolling at the end of the show. Bentley nestled in beside us for a while before he excused himself and went into the study. Mom reached over and grabbed my hand, squeezing it tightly as if to let me know everything was going to be alright. We sat for what seemed like an hour before she finally spoke, her voice gentle yet firm but pleasant.

"Are you going to that donor event tomorrow?"

"Donor event?" I had forgotten.

"Yes, remember? Two months ago, you received that invitation. I mentioned to you that it was the same night as Bentley's art fair."

"Oh, wow! Is that tomorrow tonight?" I sat up with a quickness. Where had the time gone?

"Mmm hmmm. You forgot I see."

"Mom, I have just had so much —"

"You don't have to tell me. I know you've been dealing with something that you are not talking about."

If she only knew. Her words were full of compassion, but she could see right through me. She could tell that I was struggling with something that I could not articulate. I sighed heavily, knowing that any attempt to explain would fall short of what I was actually feeling. My throat was tight as I looked upon my sweet mother's face, feeling her bond and empathy for her only daughter. I wanted to tell her everything, but I just couldn't bring myself to say the words. Instead, I simply nodded and gave her a subtle grin. In that pivotal moment, I knew how blessed I was to have her unwavering support. I felt a wave of peace wash over me like a soothing balm that whispered a fortifying reassurance.

"Take to prayer. He knows, and He protects. He is the God of all comfort." My mother's words resonated with me on a deeper level.

Remembering on all the times when I had prayed for strength and purpose, and how God had answered me despite my lack of faith. He always seemed to have an answer, even if it wasn't always easy to accept. My relationship with God differed from anything else in my life. With Him, I could honestly speak about my feelings without fear of judgement or criticism.

"Mom, you are the strongest person I know. I love you!"

Mom smiled warmly as her eyes welled up. She reached out and hugged me tightly, then gave me a tender kiss on the forehead.

"I love you too, my sweetness."

She was my rock.

Chapter Fourteen

T he sun had just risen, casting its golden light across the sky. Bentley was up earlier than usual. His mind abuzz with anticipation of the art fair he had been eagerly awaiting. Today was the day. For weeks on end, he worked tirelessly, creating, and perfecting his designs for his presentation. He poured his heart and soul into his art work. He felt sure that the judges would recognize his potential and appreciate his dedication.

"Ma, I can't wait to put my work on display tonight!" Bentley pulled out his portfolio and flipped through the pages. As he looked at each sketch, he was awe struck at their beauty. It was as if these works had come from somewhere else in time. A deeper place that only he could access. His enthusiasm was alive and infectious as he nervously paced back and forth, waiting for us to pack up the car with all of his gear.

The sky was gradually turning a deeper shade of blue, and Bentley knew the hour had arrived. He put on his coat, grabbed his portfolio, and set off. He could feel his heart beating faster with each step he took closer to the fair. The pep in his stride was obvious.

"Mom, I will meet you and Bentley at the art fair after work. Then I will pop in at the donor event for about an hour."

"Sounds good." Mom smiled.

The office was abuzz with energy and a sense of urgency emerged as donors descended from their cars and entered into the building. Men in tailored suits and women in poplin blouses and pencil skirts mingled with grateful staff members. I wrestled with the idea of telling Monica about my eerie experiences and cryptic notes. Should I? How would she react? She was inundated with charity requests, and I feared she may not be as understanding as I needed her to be.

Instead, I inquired of my colleagues whether they found our parking deck spooky or had they noticed anyone loitering about. I started at the receptionist's desk and moved from office to office, noting the puzzled expressions as I shared my experience. There were no similar stories or sightings, and it seemed that I was the only person who felt this sense of concern.

"Hope, why are you asking these weird questions? Is there something we need to know?" One co-worker inquired.

"Just curious. The garage isn't well lit, you know. Just gives me vibes." I casually responded.

"What gives you vibes?" Monica stepped out into the conversation and with an eyebrow raised in curiosity.

"Just a weird feeling I get when I'm in the garage."

"You know, Hope, you have been acting strange lately. You are always so steady and poised, it's not like you to be out of sorts. If there is something, we need to know—" Her words tapered off. Monica squinted her eyes.

"No." I was too quick to respond and spun around, walking right into Mr. Prince. The coffee cup in my hand spilled onto his three-piece suit.

"Oh! Mr. Prince! I am so deeply sorry. I am so embarrassed." Stammering as I tried to wipe the stain off his shirt with a napkin from my pocket. He gave me an unimpressed look and muttered something furiously. I could have died at that moment. Why did it have to be Mr. Prince? He was the last person I needed to burn a bridge with. He stormed off and down the hallway. For a moment, I thought of running after him, but figured it would only make matters worse.

With the donor event reception quickly approaching, without wasting another second, I snatched my briefcase and whatever remained of my dignity and rushed out the door. I had to be at Bentley's art fair in ten minutes and I was already behind schedule.

Bentley and mom arrived at the fair several minutes early and greeted the other participants. Most of them were old friends from school, but a few of them were strangers, maybe out-of-towners. It was a large gathering of two hundred exhibitors and attendees, but Bentley's confidence hadn't wavered. He knew today was his chance to introduce himself to the world as an accomplished artist. He was ready to shine.

Bentley strolled through the reception hall, taking in the various pieces of art hung on display by so many of his peers. The talent was impeccable, and Bentley could feel a hint of intimidation settling in.

Taking his place at his designated table, he hung his pieces on the wall behind him. A mix of nervousness and delight swelled within him. He'd created large multi-colored abstracts and some small, detailed sketches of city scenes. He arranged them in a way that showcased different aspects of his style and gift. The crowd filled in quickly, appreciating Bentley's breathtaking renderings. I watched as Bentley's eyes lit up when he saw the multitude of people gathered around his work. You could see how much they admired his pieces and one in particular. One close to our hearts and community.

It was time for the judges to make a decision. This was the moment we'd anticipated for so long. The judges moved closer towards Bentley's display, each one exchanging whispers and taking notes. Slowly, one by one, each judge nodded in approval of what they saw - they were impressed by Bentley's creativity and attention to detail. A few of them smiled as they pointed to his rendering of the Queen City, so beautifully illustrated as a bustling metropolis with soaring towers and vibrant markets. For Bentley, it was a symbol of hope. The promise of a bright future for a town that had long been overlooked and underestimated.

After deliberating for a while, the judges awarded him first place. Bentley couldn't believe it. Lifting his prize into the air, his eyes brimmed with tears of joy. Bentley was like a diamond that gleamed and twinkled. A sudden burst of light that pierced through the darkest clouds, now a rainbow after a long and withering storm. He was a gift and a treasure, and more than I could ever have wanted. He was a reminder that anything in this life is achievable, if only you believe in yourself.

While his gifts made him different from other children, he painted his own canvas, creating a world only visible through his eyes. It was as if he could see in the dark, and he could find a flicker where there was no flame. Bentley was truly gifted.

We took one last look around before departing, observing what remained of the momentous occasion.

Watching everyone pack up and shuffle out, hugging and laughing together, while a sense of pleasantness settled in.

"Mom, life can be good, can't it?" Bentley's eyes full of hope, I paused briefly.

"Yes, munchkin. It can."

Walking down the street, hand in hand, I reflected on how far Bentley had come in such a short amount of time - despite all that he'd lost. It seemed like only yesterday he was standing in front of me, so desperate for something to fill the void within him. And yet here we were. Walking away from an art exhibit where he'd been recognized as a gifted, creative artist — and more importantly, had the confidence to believe in himself.

"Bentley, you and mom head home. We will celebrate your victory later, after the donor event." I knelt down to his eye level and gave him a hug.

"Ok, ma." His little hands, patting me on my back.

Mom's took his hand and they headed off. But as I was walking away, I heard Bentley running up behind me.

"Ma! Ma, wait! I love you so much!" He latched on, grabbing me around the waist. My heart melted away in that moment. I turned to look into Bentley's loving brown eyes.

"I love you too, Munchkin," I whispered as I hugged him ever so tightly. We held each other in silence for a few minutes, cherishing the profound beauty of our bond. How tender and moving it was. But there was something about Bentley's expression. It was like he was saying goodbye. Almost like I wasn't ever coming back. I watched as he and mom departed before I turned away again.

Walking into the donor event, I had a queasy feeling in the pit of my stomach. It was somehow different tonight than before. My thoughts played with the elements of memory, one by one, of the way I lost Carl, my attempted murder, the black SUV, losing my dad, and the dreaded but evil Alex. I shuddered as the thoughts flashed through my mind.

Chin up, shoulders back, I pushed the thoughts aside and concluded to enjoy the evening. The night was about serving a good cause and surely, I could focus on that for one hour.

Mingling my way around the room, I forced a smile and made small talk, laughed at corny jokes, and seamlessly connected with attendees. Adorning my countenance by putting on my best face was a social skill that I had mastered to perfection. No one the wiser. With lots of salutations, hugs, and positive interchange, my performance was stellar.

"Looking good, Hope!" Monica patted me on the shoulder as she gracefully strolled past me.

Growing tired as the night moved along, my body was signaling the toll of the passing hours. Fatigue manifested like a quiet symphony, but I kept circulating, determined to meet one last group of patrons. After a brief meet and greet, I spotted several retreating guests walking towards the parking garage and joined them. Clinging to their familiarity as if it were my only defense against the malicious shadows that seemed to lurk throughout in the night. We finally reached the breezeway and said our goodbyes. I watched the group disappear into the distance and heard their voices fading away.

The air was still and quiet, with no eerie cadence of shadows withholding secrets behind every corner. I reached into my purse to get my keys, and as I did so, my thoughts turned to Bentley and Mom. I was proud of

Bentley and his pinnacle accomplishment. I marveled at how great their day had been. Feeling like we were on top of the world. I couldn't wait to get home to them and celebrate sweet Bentley.

"Where's your courage now, tramp?" Out of the shadows popped the small mysterious figure that I saw leaving the conference and the same one that hid in the parking garage's darkness among the shadows. The figure standing before me was someone I had never suspected before. Someone that took me by utter surprise.

"Janet!" I exclaimed in disbelief. With a menacing look in her eyes, she walked closer, removing the dark hood from her head. "It was you this whole time? You sending the packages and the notes? The black SUV? Why? What have I done to you?" My feet took slow, deliberate moves backwards. Janet stormed forward; her eyes wild with rage.

"Shut up, tramp, please! Spare me! I came to settle up with you!"

"Settle up on what?" I asked, still shuffling backwards. Her eyes were bloodshot, and she looked like hell. Like she hadn't slept in a week.

"Carl! You and Carl. You lived, and he died. You should have died!" She spat the words out viciously.

"Oh my God! Did you try to kill me?" I gasped.

"Shut up!" She hissed through gritted teeth, pointing a finger at me. I swallowed hard.

"Did you kill Carl?"

A twisted smile spread across Janet's face. She let out a menacing malevolent laugh.

"It was all part of my plan," she said coolly. "And I had the perfect plan!" Janet's smile widened. I could feel my heart running away as I tried to process what she was saying. My throat tightened as reality set in. "We planned it all out: the drugs, the location, the timing. Everything went according to plan. Except for you!" Janet held a manic glint in her eye.

"What drugs?" I asked but she didn't answer. My knees weakened as I tried to comprehend what she was telling me. "And now you're here because-?" Janet's expression changed from sinister amusement to icy contempt.

"Revenge," she hissed. "You and Carl ruined my life. He and his bougie little girlfriend, so wrapped up in their bubble of love. Sickening! You couldn't see how much pain you caused me!" She yelled, her eyes darkening with hatred. "So, I made it my mission to destroy you both."

Suddenly everything made sense and now Janet was standing before me - the mastermind behind this entire plot. I swallowed slowly before asking one last question, knowing this could be my only chance at getting answers.

"Who is .... we, Janet?" Janet's smile widened as she stepped closer to me. I could feel her breath as she paused and laughed. She did not answer my question so I continued, "What do you want from me, Janet?"

"I want you to pay for what Carl did," she said coldly. "Pay for destroying my life. For leaving me and being so damn happy!" She yelled viciously as her eyes took on an evil and dark fixation. She continued, her voice becoming more and more icy. "I've been planning this for months." Her voice seething with anger. "I've tracked your every move. There is nothing you have done that I don't know about."

Backed against a concrete pillar, my feet had nowhere else to go as Janet pulled out a butcher's knife from underneath her jacket. She grinned as she came closer and held the knife to my throat.

"You don't have to do this, Janet," she stopped and stared at me for a few moments before she spoke.

"You're right," she said coldly. "I don't."

My bones trembled as I saw the color drain from her skin, highlighting the dark circles under her eyes and her sharp angled features. Her eyes, once filled with malice, now looked haunted. A wave of nausea washed over me as I was confronted with the reality of her sinister plot. Janet pretending to befriend me, but she was only watching my every move.

"I really had it all figured out," she said smugly. "But you were the one variable I couldn't control. Now you will pay for ruining everything," she spat. My body flinched at the feel of the butcher knife digging into my throat. "Put these on!" she demanded.

"Where did you get handcuffs?" The wicked grin on her face was telling. She laughed at me. Frantically trying to come up with a plan of escape, my brain felt useless. I knew she was going to kill me. I tried to reason with her in one last plea.

"Please don't do this!" Janet's eyes gleamed, her tongue tracing her lips as I felt the warm blood trickle down my neck.

"It's time to collect!"

The blade of her knife digging deeper into my skin. This was my last chance to get free. It was fight or flight. I had to make my move. I struggled, trying to push the knife away from my throat. Twisting and jerking, my arm slammed painfully into a nearby car window. Janet fought back as we wrestled for control of the knife. I was able to grab Janet's arm and forcefully shove it against the fender of another car, causing her to drop the knife. Undaunted, she reached from behind her waist and pulled out a Glock five.

Tat, Tat, Tat, Tat, Tat. Sounds echoing throughout the structure. I saw Janet grab her side and fall against the wall, stumbling backwards as she took on more of the impact, but remained afoot. *Tat, Tat,* two more rounds. Janet clutched at her chest, blood trickling from her mouth, as she fell backwards off the third-floor railing to the street below.

Watching the scene unfold felt like being in the matrix, a simulation of frozen time, yet it all happened so swiftly. My vision blurred. I couldn't control the tremble in my breath. I felt my legs give out beneath me, and I collapsed to the ground.

On my knees, my eyes locked onto where Janet's body had tragically fallen from. I wiped my neckline, revealing the red blood that transferred to my hands. Unnerved, I rose to my feet, my movements mechanical and slow, and proceeded towards the ledge.

As I peered over the side, a shiver crept down my back like an icy hand. There, in the street below, lay Janet's lifeless body. I stared at her with a numbness, not of sorrow but a surreal disbelief, like I couldn't feel anything at all.

"Is she....is she dead?" A voice whispered over my shoulder.

"You? Of all the people! I never would've thought." I stood there holding my throat.

"Yes, Hope. I have been watching you from afar and for a very long time. I know what happened to you at the hands of Alex, and I have seen your struggle to survive, knowing there was nothing I could do for you. This, tonight, I can do for you!"

"But, how did you know about Janet's plot?" I was stunned.

"It doesn't matter now." Detective Thomas's voice softened.

"I don't know what to say." I just stared at the man I knew as a highly regarded law enforcer.

"Nothing suits me just fine."

We stared down at the stillness of Janet's body as she lay motionless on the street below. The sound of tires screeching and sirens wailing in the distance filled the air, drowning out any other noise. Without a word the detective took off his jacket and draped it over my shoulders. I shivered at the sudden warmth, but also at the realization of his selflessness. He looked into my eyes, which were reddened and glassy with tears. Lightly touching my arm in a gesture of comfort, he gave me a scarf for my neck.

Shifting his gaze away and surveying the area, he directed his attention to the aftermath that surrounded us. He took a few steps forward, his eyes carefully scanning the ground for shell casings.

"What do we do now?" My voice was trembling in the night air. The detective took a deep breath, cautiously looking around, packing his gun into its holster.

"We wait!" He said firmly. "The police will be here soon, and I will tell them what happened to you. It was all in self-defense."

Nodding, with tears trickling down my face. I knew Detective Thomas pulled the trigger to save my life. His face, all sweaty and crinkled, as he reached for my hand.

"You are very lucky, Ms. Everly."

"I wouldn't call it luck. God is with me. My faith is in Him."

Nodding in approval, he took out his keys and released the handcuffs from my wrists. The unspoken dialogue between us undeniable.

It was done.

As we waited for the police to arrive, a feeling of dreadfulness settled deep into my gut. I knew I was fortunate to be alive, and finally the nightmare was over but wondered, would the detective get into trouble? I watched as he walked down the exit ramp to meet the incoming cars.

When the police arrived, they questioned me suspiciously as I recounted the events of the evening. Two officers leaned in closer with rapt attention. I could feel their doubt and apprehension when they exchanged glances with each other. It felt as if my words were put under a magnifying glass for scrutinizing. Their intense gazes made me feel like I was being picked apart piece by piece.

"Ma'am, who shot your attacker?" The officer's eyes shifted to his notepad. I remained silent.

"Do you know your assailant?" His voice calm but firm.

"Unfortunately, I do." With a hard swallow I answered.

"Ms. Everly, you do know how this looks, don't you?" With suspicion in his voice, the Chief walked over to join us.

"Maybe you would like to tell me what you haven't told the officer?"

"Chief, I suggest you speak with Detective Thomas, ABI." The Chief's gaze snapped up to meet my own. I could see the intensity of his bewilderment.

"ABI?" he questioned.

"Yes, Chief." Detective Thomas replied as he approached us from the left. The Chief seemed taken aback by the sudden ABI presence pulling rank but nodded in respect.

I watched as the police went about their business efficiently and professionally, combing every aspect of the crime scene for evidence and clues. They dusted for fingerprints and took photographs from various angles while questioning people that gathered outside the tapped perimeter close by.

When they were finished, the officer in charge gave me a curt nod. I couldn't help feeling relieved, but I was also a little apprehensive about what would happen next. One officer was generous enough to bring me a cup of coffee. With shaking hands, I tried to steady the cup to take a sip. I took deep breaths to calm my nerves, but it didn't seem to help much.

"Ms. Everly, you are free to leave, but don't leave town," the Chief said gruffly as he handed me a business card. He then turned away and began a sidebar with Detective Thomas. The expressions they exchanged were confusing to me. I tried to read the body language but found no answers in what I saw.

"Hey, I thought you said there was a body?" Another attending officer asked.

"Yes, just over the edge." Detective Thomas pointed to the area.

As we walked over to the spot where Janet fell, I took a deep breath. My stomach refused to look at Janet's body, but something else inside me wanted one last confirmation that she was dead. I leaned over the side of the concrete barrier and pointed downward.

"She fell right — "

Every muscle in my body reverberated. My eyes were looking upon the scene where the body fell but Janet was gone. Nothing was left but a few drops of blood on the concrete below.

"How could that be? I saw her lifeless body!" I just stood there staring at the emptiness below.

As the officers surveyed the scene, the body was nowhere in sight. With silent communication through exchanged glances, one of the officers spoke up, prompting further action.

"Call Forensics."

Detective Thomas exchanged a concerning look with me and shook his head. Gesturing for us to step away from the area, he placed his hand on my shoulder, gently nudging me away for the ledge. My body drooped as I sat down on the curb. Detective Thomas knelt beside me, and we remained like that for a few moments before the Chief towered over us.

"Is there something else you'd like to tell me, Ms. Everly?" he asked gently. I shook my head in confusion, not trusting my voice to work properly. He stood and motioned for an officer to come over. "See that Ms. Everly gets an escort home."

Trembling and weak, I stumbled to my feet with the officer's help when my eyes met with Monica's. Her face was alive with so many feelings and emotions, her skin flushed with a deep, rosy hue. The emotions on her face only made the guilt in my chest expand until I could no longer hold her gaze and had to look away. Monica's face emitted shock as she tried to grasp the chaos.

All the work I put in. All those years, to hide behind my newfound success and keep locked away my book of painful secrets, now out in the open. Leaving me exposed to the world for all to examine my plight. The plunder of my greatest treasures trashed at the hands of Janet. Though she may not have completely accomplished her mission, she dismantled my life and unearthed my existence. But, at least, I still had my life.

Searching around for a way out of the intense air that smothered me, I saw the all too familiar looks of judgment from the faces that surrounded me in the night. It was as if I could feel their thoughts, uncovering my intricate layers, and penetrating my soul. Over my left shoulder I could feel Monica's stares burning holes in the detective's jacket, still draped around my weary body, cradling my arms, and covering my hands.

The police combed the area for any sign of Janet as my mind raced with scenarios. I saw her fall three stories and lay lifeless on the street below. Who could get up from that? Was she still alive?

Leaving the scene of the crime feeling traumatized, sorting, and compartmentalizing my life, I couldn't help but tell Jehovah God thank you for being there one more time. For seeing me, for hearing me, for saving me, for never letting go of my right hand. For saving Bentley's mom.

Chapter Fifteen

T hree months later.

The police never found Janet. Monica and the board decided I was no longer a good fit for the organization and asked me to resign.

Mr. Prince withdrew his offer, and I spent the next year living off my savings, working at the family business, and going back to school.

In the Fall of my postgrad year, I landed an executive position at a Fortune 500 company while finishing my master's degree at Harvard.

Bentley and I moved into an affluent neighborhood on the sun-drenched east coast, where the palm trees lined the landscape and the streets echoed with prosperity. Bentley was thriving and grew into a daringly handsome young man, head of his class and was awarded the National Medal of Artistry among his peers.

Our days unfolded in the opulent embrace of a new life. A new story to write and a new chapter to begin. We could finally put the brutal past to rest and unpack our new adventures.

We put miles and memories behind us with love and faith between us. A shared flame, weaving a new chapter of warmth and connection, turning the remnants of rising smoke into the sparks of a vibrant, shared odyssey.

For the shadows of the night befall us –
but she that believes shall rise.
Rise up out of the ashes like smoke-
becoming sparks and embers, electrified.
Her light is her beauty, her fire no longer hides.
She belongs to the Life Giver-
The Redeemer has restored her life.

Chapter Sixteen

T wo years later.

Sun coast living was warm and breezy, always tempting you outside into the rays of light that beckoned your attention to a different way of life. A new life that was almost everything I'd ever wished for and today was the day that I celebrated me.

"Ms. Everly, I believe that you'd much prefer the Volvo over the Mercedes." The car salesman, sporting an Emporio suit, approached with a confident grin and squinty beagle eyes.

"I need something reliable, fuel efficient, equipped with the highest safety rating, along with a measure of class." I stated as I slid my sunglasses off my face.

"Picture this, a modern sedan with innovative tech, smooth handling, and fuel efficiency. How does that grab you?" The sun seemed to bounce off his forehead like tiny beams of light.

"Sir, I wasn't looking for it to grab me at all, and I am not looking for a sedan."

"I have just what you want!" He winked his eye and raised his brow. His grin reminded me of the grinch, hinting at a mischievous charm that added a playful twist to the otherwise serious business of car sales. "What color would you like?"

He led the way to a showroom with black-and-white checkered flooring, glossed with a mirror-like shine that reflected the allure of the sleek vehicles showcased within it. We walked across the showroom and out the side glass doors to the north lot of the dealership.

There she sat, glistening in the sun, as she exuded elegance, polished in chrome with an eye dazzling Saville silver appearance. Each curve and detail spoke of opulence, inviting admiration under the radiant blue sky. A sanctuary of black leather interior with a scent of sophistication blended with a cocoon of comfort. The engine purred with precision and power, a prowess of refinement in every rev of the motor.

"This will do just fine, sir." I adorned.

"Will this be cash or finance?" His teeth sparkled as the words flowed effortlessly from his lips.

"Finance, for now." I'd never been able to afford anything so opulent, but with everything I'd been through, it was time I commemorated my victory with a new car. Stepping into a new realm of luxury, this was a testament to triumph over adversity and a celebration long overdue.

Waiting for the ink to dry on the title work, I gazed out the window at the seagulls soaring in flight. The sun, a fiery orb, cast its golden glow over the horizon, painting the atmosphere in shades of orange and pink. The dazzle of sunlight manifested feelings of gratitude as I recalled the broken road that brought me to this pinnacle moment.

"Ms. Everly, we should finish up everything in about fifteen minutes." The finance manager confirmed.

"Thank you." I responded as I retrieved my cell phone to check in at the office. We had some major clients coming in this week and the thought of closing a big deal filled me with anticipation. This deal would secure a new venture for me and elevate my career to new heights.

Among my clients were doctors, lawyers, retired yacht owners, CEOs, and real estate moguls. My firm was branching out into the global sector of billing modernization and business assets management, weaving a tapestry of financial excellence across diverse industries. There had been some suggestive language around the office of the firm reaching a deal with a major player in the nonprofit sector, but that had not been confirmed and I was not going to get involved with that one.

"Ms. Everly, your shiny new ride is ready for you." Those words had a jingle that energized my spirit.

"Thank you." I could barely contain my excitement, eager to pick up my munchkin and go for a spin around town.

Amidst the luxurious comfort and seamless adaptive suspension, I almost felt a bit unworthy somehow. It was a harmonious contradiction where self-affirmation met the novelty of a lifestyle not yet woven into the fabric of my everyday existence. But, with determination coursing through my veins, I pressed the accelerator, feeling the power beneath my snakeskin stilettos translating into a surge of controlled energy.

"Yasssssss!" my lips celebrated. The road unfolded before me, a canvas of newfound confidence in every press of the pedal.

Bentley had no idea of my surprise and upon arriving at his school, I saw him scanning the line of vehicles for our old, tired SUV with the broken side mirror and missing hubcaps. Once I caught his gaze, I stepped out of my vehicle and waved, motioning for him to walk over and reveal our upgraded chariot. His face overflowing with astonishment, Bentley dashed over to greet me, enveloping me with his warm hugs and brimming smile.

"Oh Wow, Ma! This is so awesome. Is this yours?"

"It is! Get in."

With every turn around town, he was intrigued by the lux feel and quiet ride of our new car. We opened the sunroof and let in the coastal breeze.

"Hey, want to hear something special?" I winked.

"Sure, ma." His excitement only sparked my enthusiasm. I could hardly hold it in.

"This car... is a Bentley!" We laughed and laughed so hard until I thought my sides would burst.

"That is too funny, ma!"

We rounded the corner to our neighborhood, streets perfectly landscaped with colorful floral assortments. Bright pinks, purples, whites, and yellows lined the street from one end to the other. It almost felt too perfect, like a postcard or a dream. I could smell the sweet scent of the flowers in the air, and it made me feel giddy with joy.

We continued to laugh and talk. I kept looking around, taking everything in. The sun was still shining, birds were singing, and it seemed like the world was in perfect harmony. I felt so alive and full of life, like I could do anything I wanted.

Pulling into our driveway, we waved at our neighbor out tending to his petunias, his wife looking on as to applaud our fresh addition to the family. I sat there for a moment admiring our new home and taking in the details of how pristine everything looked. Our brownstone brick veneer home presented a sense of warmth and coziness that made us feel welcomed and safe. The automatic garage door opened, and I drove inside, parking near our kitchen entrance.

Upon entry there was a large island in the middle of the room, with counters and shelves on either side for extra storage space. There was a spacious office down the hallway and off the living area, which I decorated with cherry wood and Queen Anne pieces from a local antique dealer.

Upstairs were four bedrooms and four bathrooms, a rec room, and a study lined with literary works that Bentley and I long admired. We could sit for hours reading and getting lost in other worlds, past and present. It was those books that helped us escape some difficult times in our lives, offering solace and companionship, like cherished old friends.

In the middle of our study library, was our favorite book displayed on a podium out of the two hundred books we had collected. A silver, soft matte covered masterpiece with thin delicate white paper pages reflecting the reverence associated with the brilliance within it. This sacred testament of holy writings, proudly on display exhibiting the faith we found in God and his place in our lives that we so humbly cherished.

Downstairs in the kitchen, Bentley turned on every light we had illuminating the space with a soft warm glow that cast a comfortable atmosphere, inviting us to just sit and bask in the splendor. On the counter was a fresh bouquet of fragrant flowers, a gift from our loved ones, with its vibrant hues exuding joy and positive vibes.

As Bentley pulled out a bag of chips from the pantry, I reached for two glasses and filled them with cold sparkling cider from the fridge. We meandered towards the living room still laughing at our little joke, just enjoying each other's presence in gentle silence as we savored life's simple pleasures. We settled into our favorite sofa to watch TV and laugh at silly sitcoms until it was time for bed. Bentley trotted upstairs as I sat down at my desk to check emails before turning in for the evening.

Sifting through my inbox, I noticed one email that stood out from the other seventy-five unread messages. Familiar was the name of the sender, and my interest was piqued by the subject line: "Meeting at 9am - Investment Prospects in Emerging Markets." Apparently, the suggestive language around the office of the firm reaching a new deal wasn't just talk, after all.

The next morning, I arrived at the office early and made my way up to the conference room. The atmosphere was hushed with anticipation, not a whisper in the room. Tim, our CEO, opened the meeting by introducing a few corporate partners who had expressed keen interest in our newest venture. We then heard their pitch and learned more about how our company could benefit from their collaboration.

"There is one new partner that I am most excited about, and I have decided to appoint someone to assist with our biggest project to date. I am confident that the person selected will dominate in this role, securing our firm's place in this new partnership." Tim pronounced. "Hope Everly!" His voice was alive with energy. Stunned, I couldn't believe his choice on such an outstanding initiative. Truly honored, I rose to my feet as my peers congratulated me and Tim shook my hand with acceptance.

"Hope, I want you to meet our new business partner. The two of you will, no doubt, work closely together and collaborate on this deal. I am counting on you, Hope."

My face was on fire with elation as I turned to greet our new partner and colleague.

"Meet Mr. Louis Monroe of The Monroe Group."

I felt all the air leave my body when my eyes met his intense gaze. A wave of inflamed heat seared through me. I stood there recalling our last encounter and the words he spoke to me, lingering in the air like an echo of bittersweet memories. The intensity of being confronted with a face from a life that I left far behind was like a sudden collision of past and present mixed with nostalgia and unresolved emotions. It had been years since I last saw Louis Monroe, but his timeless charm and allure created a bittersweet blend of familiarity and the realization of some things unchanged.

Louis wore a knowing smirk that hinted at a covert secret, adding an intriguing layer of mystery to his arrival. Leaving me feeling like this was a scripted reunion orchestrated without my knowledge.

With Tim and the entire team looking on, I composed myself and extending my hand as if Louis and I were meeting for the very first time. He took my hand and squeezed gently, his eyes never leaving mine. In that moment, it felt like time rewound, suspended between regret and feelings I wasn't ready to explore.

"Tim, I am sure that Ms. Everly and I will work beautifully together. I know I am looking forward to it."

There was something about the way Louis radiated when speaking those words that made me weak. Why did he have to come back into my life, disrupting the harmony I'd come to cherish, and why now? I loved my life the way it was, and Louis was just a reminder of the past that I deliberately left behind.

Adjourning the meeting, Tim leaned in and whispered over my left shoulder on his way out of the room. "I am counting on you. Play nice."

I nodded and looked over to Louis, who was sitting at the head of the conference table. His gaze was fervent, never wavering from mine, as if he was trying to convey something powerful through his eyes. Upon the close of the conference room door, I sat on the edge of the table with a laser focus on Louis's relaxed stance.

"What in the hell, Louis?"

"Good heavens, you are more beautiful than I ever remember. You've lost weight, and you have a glow that simply commands my attention. Your hair is different too, but I like it." He was stroking my nerves.

"How did you find me?" My blood was boiling up. He stood and walked over.

"You know, I remember when you asked me that same question back at that nonprofit, what was it, When Our World Changes?"

"Our World is Changing," I meticulously corrected.

"Yes, that place." He smirked. "Look, it is no secret. I have always kept tabs on you. What can I say? You mean something to me, Hope. Something that I felt the very first moment that I saw you, like nothing I have ever felt for anyone. You're under my skin. So, I researched this firm you work for and, ironically, this company aligns with where I am going with my nonprofit. Call it fate."

"Fate?" Walking away from Louis, I shook my head at his serendipitous suggestion.

"Hope, no one is chasing you anymore. Well, except for me," he laughed.

"You find that funny, do you?" With my hand on my hips, I turned to walk away.

"Hey, I am not making light of your past, but what I am saying is that you have built quite a new life for yourself here, and lady, I am so proud of you. You are stronger than anyone I know. You are amazing, to say the least."

I felt all confidence seep away when my eyes met his commanding gaze, a moment suspended in time that carried the weight of unspoken affections and unexplored possibilities. If I allowed myself to get lost in his charm, I would have been blindsided by the emotions that were stirring within me. His presence brought up forgotten feelings, and I was reminded how smooth he could be with his eloquence.

"This is just business, Louis." I picked up my briefcase and turned only for Louis to catch my arm.

"Still running, I see," he proclaimed. "Why do I scare you so much?" His words struck me. I struggled to answer.

"You want a collaborative partner in this firm, so be it. I will be that, but nothing more." I turned away from him but found myself asking, why *was* I scared?

"Are you afraid of finding love again or afraid of the possibility of losing it again?"

My eyes quickly cut to his and I could tell from his expression that he read me like a book. He knew he had struck a nerve with that careless innuendo.

"Hope, I'm sorry for being so blunt." His apology seemed sincere enough, but I was over it. I strutted towards the door with a regal demeanor. Seeing my reflection in the large glass doors on my way out, I paused for a moment to deliver closure.

"I will send you a link to my calendar and you can propose some dates for us to work on your venture. And no, before you ask, I am not open to dinner."

The next few months with Louis were fraught with tension as he served up his charming smile and endless compliments. His eyes would flicker, trying to keep the conversations lingering longer than appropriate, testing the boundaries that I'd set for him. He always played the Alpha, and I let him; anything to appease his hungry ego and get the project completed on time.

Louis tried to extend our working hours into the night, but I was clear on my timeline and my responsibilities to Bentley. Though he never gave up trying, he was at least understanding, and that was one quality I richly admired about him. I had deadlines to meet, reports to write, and meetings to attend.

On the days when he seemed particularly frustrated or annoyed with me, I often wondered if there was anything else going on behind the scenes that he wasn't telling me about. Was it just his own issues with perfectionism impeding our progress or his selfish desire to win? Still, he kept a positive attitude and maintained his optimism most of the time.

The partnership was a beautiful dance, each step in perfect synchrony, a delightful harmony of the minds, pushing each other to get better results. His attention to detail and commitment to excellence were something else that made him stand out. We even shared laughter over a funny situation or story, though it rarely lasted longer than a few minutes before his gaze wandered, and I would have to remind him to stay on task.

Louis Monroe had always been a visionary, a brilliant businessman, a diligent strategist. His reputation preceded him, an attestation to his unwavering commitment and foresight that fueled my admiration of him as I considered the history we shared. I just couldn't believe that we shared enough outside of the business commonality and physical attraction to have a future together, although I wondered. Would we ever dare to find out?

The end of the Summer was approaching and so was the end of my oversight and mutual partnership collaboration with The Monroe Group. I even circled the date on my calendar and reminded Louis of it. It was marking not only the conclusion of a season but also the inevitable shift in the dynamic of our mutual quests.

"Hope, come away with me!" Louis insisted. "Leave this firm and come join me at The Monroe Group." He brushed up to me, taking my hands in his, so close I could feel every syllable of every word he spoke.

"Louis, it would never work." His eyes held mine captive.

"You were meant to be a leader, Hope, not to work for someone else helping them build their empire. You are ready." His words resonated with a subtle call for me to look inside myself for my purpose and vision.

"Louis, I have enjoyed working with you on this project and I wish you all the best that life offers you. It's just that my path differs from yours, always has, and all I ask is that you respect that." I could see a hint of affection on his face, and he nodded in understanding as he stepped closer, closing any space left between us.

"Hope," he whispered. "You have immense potential. Don't let anyone or anything stand in your way of achieving your dreams, ever." His words were filled with generosity and a tender warmth of care. It was then that I realized how much our partnership had meant to both of us, but also how much Louis Monroe really cared about Hope Everly.

As Louis released my hands and took three steps back, he gazed at me like we'd never see each other again. I felt like a part of me was going with him as he gathered his fedora and leather briefcase, giving me a wink and a smile before leaving to catch his flight back home.

In the weeks that followed our departure, Tim promoted me to Chief Operating Officer of our firm. I moved into a massive corner office overlooking the bay area. The sparkling waters stretched out before me, dotted with sailboats, and bustling with activity. The city skyline loomed in the distance, a sprawling metropolis of towering buildings and bustling streets. And above it all, the clear blue sky stretched out endlessly, inviting, and expansive. The view was breathtaking. I could stare at it for hours, watching the gulls soar and swoop against the vibrant backdrop. Sometimes my mind drifted to Louis, wondering how he was doing and if he ever thought about me.

My workday always began with a caramel macchiato and endless emails. My secretary, Sandra Watson, would bring in the stack of correspondence from the mail room downstairs and sort it by level of importance. Rarely did anything exciting come from the mailroom. Sandra would sift out the boring letters for me, one by one, but today was different. Sandra looked up from her stack.

"Here is an interesting envelope. Looks important." She stood there with her lips pressed together. I stopped clicking away at the keyboard to see the curious look on her face.

"Who is it from?"

Sandra never spoke a word. She placed the white envelope on top of my keyboard in front of me and slowly exited my office. She paused, taking a last glance before closing the door behind her. With the white envelope beckoning my attention, I carefully examined the outside of it. Sender: The Monroe Group.

I brushed my fingers lightly over the envelope, notic-
ing the perfectly placed penmanship that I easily recognized as Louis Monroe's. It had been months since we
parted ways, not so much as a phone call and yet here was
an envelope addressed to me.

I was filled with avidity. I carefully opened the envelope, not wanting to ruin any of its contents, to pre-
serve any measure of what he'd touched. Inside were
several neatly folded pages of handwritten letters, and my
heart leapt with excitement as I eagerly read each one.
His penmanship was elegant and exhibited grace. Each
stroke unfolded a precision of sophistication almost like
timeless art. Louis' letters detailed his own journey of
self-discovery since our parting and included photos of
him overseas at his newly renovated branch office.

His story and eloquent words were inspiring and up-
lifting, breathing life into the pages, giving me inspiration to keep pushing towards my own goals in life. He
closed out the letter with a simple request: "*My darling
Hope, do whatever it takes to find true happiness, and in doing
so, build your own empire.*" He then added two final words:
"*stop running.*"

Seated in solitude, I was sinking into a sea of emotions. His request was like ripples on the bay that stirred
the fluidity of my soul. Resting the beautifully written
letters atop my desk, I looked inside the envelope once
more. What I found was a small blue note card with an
aroma of Dolce, blank on the outside, carefully detailed
on the inside, that read: "*If only they were as stunning as
you, my darling.*" If only what? I held the envelope upside
down, shaking it as if something else must have been
stuck inside it.

"Excuse me, Hope." Sandra trotted in. "You have a
delivery." Her voice danced in the air.

"Ok, so deliver it." I spoke so uncaringly. Still probing the envelope for answers.

"No, I mean you have a *delivery!*" I stopped and stared at her.

"What is wrong with you today, Sandra? You're acting like a schoolgirl."

The delivery came rolling in on carts. One by one, they came filling up every corner of my massive office space. Elaborate bouquets of roses; pink, white, red, yellow; roses everywhere. I couldn't believe my eyes as the bouquets flooded in until, finally, they completely covered the floor.

"What is all this?" I asked Sandra breathlessly.

"You'll never guess who sent all these flowers!" She answered with a smirk on her face.

"I can't imagine." I ventured forth to read the card that was tucked away inside one of the largest bouquets. Another blue card that read: *"If only they were as beautiful as you, my darling."* ~ Louis

Silent yet brimming with emotion, my words held no audible presence. I lifted my gaze to meet Sandra's enthusiastic eyes. My whole day was upended by Louis's incredible surprise. The otherwise busy office, now filled with the sweet aroma of roses, was still and quiet. Colleagues came flooding in. Their unified gasps of adornment created a harmonious choir, echoing with the sentiments of someone's affection.

My heart was full, but my mind was a whirlwind, overflowing with a million different questions about Louis Monroe. I couldn't help but wonder what his intentions were with this grand gesture. Was it a genuine act of kindness, or a ploy to win me over? As much as I wanted to believe in the former, I couldn't release the feeling that there was something more behind it. Louis was clearly a man determined to win in every aspect of his life. Yet, the splendor of his thoughtfulness was bountiful and spread out before me to adorn.

As the week ended, Friday made its quiet entrance. The air was thick with the heady scent of roses, their soft petals creating a vibrant and overpowering display. Although exquisite in bloom, I knew they'd soon begin to wilt. In a show of appreciation, I asked Sandra to share the beauties with our dedicated team on the 15th floor.

With a beaming smile, Sandra eagerly set off to collect the roses, placing each vase onto a rolling cart. I could hear the soft rustling of petals as each staff member collected their own vase full of luscious blooms. They were all overjoyed to partake in the grandeur of my magnificent garden.

Sandra's heels clicked against the marble floors as she reentered the room. She swung her leather-bound notebook and planner in one hand while balancing my afternoon tea in the other.

"You have a meeting at 2:00, a photo opp at 3:00, and Tim wants you to RSVP for the annual gala by 5:00pm today." Sandra, my tireless assistant, and keeper of my schedule, was a well-oiled machine, never failing to keep me on track and organized.

"Gala?" I furrowed my brows, trying to recall when the gala was supposed to be. Time had a way of creeping up on me, especially with all the demands that Tim placed on my shoulders. He was probably somewhere on the golf course by now.

"Yes, Hope. You know how Tim gets."

"Okay," I replied, nodding my head in understanding. "But first, lunch."

Sandra gave me a knowing smile, understanding my need for sustenance before tackling a day full of meetings and obligations. I couldn't help but feel grateful for her presence and efficiency. Without her, I would surely be lost, both literally and figuratively. She not only kept my schedule in check, but she also provided a sense of stability and structure in my otherwise chaotic work life.

Grabbing my purse, I headed out for a quick meal at the corner café. The air carried a salty breeze and the aroma of freshly cooked seafood mingled with the inviting scent of flavorful dishes that delighted my palate. The clinking of dishes and glasses drew my attention as I entered the café. A delightful symphony in the background as silverware chimed against plates when stacked. It felt like a cozy and familiar place, where people gathered to share a meal and catch up with each other's lives.

Feeling all caught up in my moment of bliss, the sound of my cell phone vibrating broke through my thoughts. I reluctantly pulled it out of my pocket, not recognizing the number on the screen. A part of me wanted to ignore it and continue basking in the warm atmosphere of the café, but a nagging feeling tugged at me. What if it was an important call?

With a sigh, I answered and held the phone to my ear. It seemed like just another interruption in an already tumultuous day. The persistent vibration pulled me away from my lunch, my musings, and my carefully constructed world.

"Hello?" I answered, trying to keep the irritation out of my voice. "Hello?" There was no answer. I could hear some shuffling and muffled voices in the background. It sounded like someone was trying to speak but faltered. My frustration grew as the silence continued. "Can you hear me? Who is this?" I asked, annoyed at the prank call or telemarketer on the other end. "Dang telemarketers!"

I glanced at the clock and saw it was almost 1:00pm, so I grabbed my wallet and headed back to the office.

The bustling street was filled with people as they hurried past me, chatting, and laughing while the sun beat down on their faces. The sunlight danced about, playing with the reflections against my eyes, creating an interplay of memories about Carl and fast forwarding to Louis. I shook my head, trying to regain my focus. A distraction that I did not need at the moment, but as I continued walking, my mind wandered back to that call.

"Where are you going?" That voice. I halted in my tracks. Scanning the street for the source of the voice that had just called out to me. People were strolling past me, but no one in particular stood out.

"Hello?" I called out, feeling ridiculous for talking to thin air. After a few more moments of looking around, I continued down the sidewalk. I exhaled. Maybe it was just my imagination playing tricks on me. How weird.

After a few more blocks, the phone call was still lingering in my mind. Something about the day felt off. As much as I tried to dismiss it as nothing, something about it didn't feel right. Was it just a wrong number? Or was someone trying to reach me? But as I turned down another street, that voice called out to me again.

"Where are you going?" The voice sounded different this time. It was deeper and more distinct. And it sounded like it was coming from somewhere close by. I slowly turned in a circle, scanning my surroundings for anyone who might be there.

I squinted into the sunlight, straining to see through the brightness. The hair on my neck prickled as I asked, "Who's there?"

Silence greeted me. I scanned the street corner for any sign of life. My heart pounded in my chest as I wondered if I was going crazy.

"Ok, Hope, get yourself together." Giving myself a pep talk and swiftly moving towards the office, my heels were clicking faster on the pavement.

Rounding the corner to meet the streamlined contemporary architecture of my firm's lofty tower, I hurried inside to the glass elevator. Inside the quietness, I took deep breaths of release as I felt the safety of the familiar surroundings. I leaned back against the cool glass walls, closed my eyes, and let out a sigh of contentment.

The elevator began its ascent, and with every floor, I felt the weight of the day falling away. The city below became smaller and smaller. A distant memory as the sleek and modern interior of the tower surrounded me. The elevator doors slid open with a soft hiss, revealing the bustling scene of the 15th floor. It was the epicenter of all important company decisions.

As I stepped out, I was immediately startled by Tim, with his briefcase in hand. His salt-and-pepper hair was neatly combed back, and his tailored suit made him appear even more commanding than usual.

"Hope, be sure to RSVP to the gala by 5:00 today," he said in his usual brisk tone. "Your presence is important. We need to show the clients that we are a united front."

I nodded, already mentally adding it to my to-do list. Besides, there was no way Sandra was going to let me forget about it. Her organizational skills were impeccable, and she was detailed right down to the minute.

"Hope, Sandra is looking for you." The front desk receptionist always greeted me with her welcoming smile.

"Of course." I returned the gesture and headed towards my office, passing by colleagues who were diligently working at their desks. The fluorescent lights flickered above, casting a sickly pallor over everything. My forehead began to sweat, and my stomach felt queasy, as if the fluorescent lights were burning a hole through me.

Without a word to anyone, I darted into the ladies' room to freshen up and gather myself. But even there, I couldn't rid myself of the feeling of being trapped. The tight stalls and sterile surroundings only added to the mounting sense of claustrophobia. I wondered if I could make it through the day without having a panic attack.

I turned on the faucet and began splashing cold water onto my face while still trying to push away the overwhelming feelings of pressure and stress. What was happening to me? I patted my face dry and leaned into the sink, steadying myself for balance.

I stepped into the hallway and off to the breakroom, just hoping to get a seltzer to settle my stomach. The cool air from the overhead vent seemed to soothe my skin as I sat alone for at least fifteen minutes. The breakroom was dimly lit and a welcome contrast to the bright and busy office. I sank into a chair at the small round table in the corner, at the back of the room.

"Hope, there you are. I have been looking for you." Sandra found me; her voice was urgent. She had with her a crisp navy-blue folder labeled: Monroe Project. "Tim wanted me to give you this and ask that you familiarize yourself with the details of your upcoming meeting."

Of course he did, I thought. "Sure thing." I gave her a gentle nod as I stared at the label. Who could escape Louis Monroe? He might as well assume an office at the firm.

"Hope, I almost forgot." Sandra spun around and pointed to the door. "You have a visitor. He looks important, like White House important." She smirked and waited for my reaction. Just what I needed, an unexpected visitor.

"Can you show him to my office?"

Before Sandra could answer, in walked a face from the past. My hand unconsciously reached for the edge of the table, fingers nervously tapping on the smooth surface. The air suddenly felt thick, as if a forgotten memory had been brought to life. Before me, there he stood.

"Detective Thomas!" The words leapt out of my mouth before I could think to stop them.

"Hello Ms. Everly."

Shocked out of my mind, I stared for a moment before I asked Sandra to leave us. The detective towered over me, his tall frame seemingly taking up most of the space. His black suit was perfectly pressed and his beard, neatly trimmed, conformed to his jawline.

"You always seem to make quite an entrance." I joked nervously.

"Ms. Everly, let's get straight to the point here." His voice was stern and unyielding. "We have identified the person responsible for Carl's death."

My heart stopped. I had been waiting for this moment, dreading it but also desperate for closure. I couldn't believe it was finally happening.

"Who?" I asked, my voice barely above a whisper. The detective paused for a moment, as if he was gathering his thoughts. I could feel my heart racing, my palms growing sweaty. I couldn't bear the suspense any longer. "Who did it?" I just knew he was going to say Janet. After all, she practically admitted it.

"We have evidence that points to one person in particular. It was Alex." His words hit like a punch in the gut. I felt my knees start to buckle as the truth sank in. Thoughts and memories of Alex flooded forth.

"So, he is in custody then?" I felt a degree of fear begin to swell.

"We picked him up this morning." His face was grim and serious. I took a deep breath in trying to calm my thoughts. I wasn't shocked by the news but somehow, I wasn't completely satisfied.

"Why? What was the motive?" A brief pause filled the air. He lowered his head before continuing.

"There is still so much I cannot say due to the nature of the case," his voice low and serious. His demeanor was guarded, his words carefully chosen. There was a tension in the air, like a taut wire waiting to snap. I could feel my frustration growing. I needed answers, and I needed them now.

"What about Janet?" I asked, desperation creeping into my voice.

"We're still investigating," he replied, his face betraying nothing. "No trace of her. We have been searching for—" he trailed off. I could tell there was more he wanted to say. But he remained silent, a brick wall between me and the truth. "Her whereabouts and if she is still alive," he concluded. "I'm sorry." His voice strained. "I wish I could give you more information."

I couldn't quite put my finger on it, but I had a nagging feeling that there was more to the story than the detective was letting on.

"Thank you for telling me." I said softly. "But why did you come all this way to deliver the news? I mean, you could have called. Obviously, you knew how to reach me."

"I wanted to make sure you were aware of the situation since Carl was your fiancé and I needed to tell you in person." His eyes said more to me than his mouth was delivering.

"While I do appreciate that, I get the feeling there is more?"

The detective's head tilted to the side, his face contorting into a confused and slightly concerned expression. His eyebrows tensed and his eyes fixed, showing surprise or maybe even worry. His usually straight posture seemed to soften, and his face took on a contemplative expression.

"I just wanted you to know, and I will be in touch if there is anything further. Here is my card if need me." Sliding the card across the table, he then stood to walk away but paused briefly.

"Ms. Everly, it is good to see how much you've overcome. The way, well, you have adjusted. Most people would find it difficult to start over after what you have experienced. Stay strong." He gave me a nod and disappeared into the hallway.

I tasted a bitterness on my tongue as I meditated on his words. I sat in silence and confusion. His business card lay on the table in front of me where my eyes noticed something different about it. The emblem of the FBI was printed in bold letters at the top, followed by his full name and title: *Special Agent, Albert Thomas.*

My hands were shaking as I turned it over to see his contact information on the back. FBI? What connection did the FBI have to this? I tucked the business card into my pocket before gathering my belongings. It was time to return to my office and get ready for the meetings scheduled in the afternoon. I was sure that Tim would be checking for my RSVP.

My charming workspace welcomed me with the scent of roses still lingering in the air. Beckoning me in with its sweet fragrance and tender warmth. The rays of sunshine pouring in lifted my spirits, momentarily pushing aside the jaw dropping news. Louis's voice echoed in my mind, his laughter still ringing in my ears. My heart was aflutter with emotions and my mind confused by feelings and encounters. Mixed with the day's events made for the perfect storm of hope and despair. I studied on the unraveling of Carl's death at the hands of Alex and wondered what his motive had been.

Just as I was delving deeper into dissecting the mystery, Sandra glided into the room. Her hands were balancing a small mountain of letters and a delicate silver tray with my usual afternoon tea. I inhaled deeply, letting the aroma of steaming jasmine and honey surround me before taking a careful sip. The heat soothed my nerves as the fragrant flavors danced around on my tongue.

Sandra rested a few legal documents on my desk atop the navy blue folder that called to me. Its vibrant hue beckoning like a siren's song amidst the sea of beige and gray stacks of paperwork. But it was the rather large white envelope underneath it that caught my attention. My face radiated with wonder like the first hints of a sunrise, just knowing who it was from. Butterflies swirled inside my stomach and my hands trembled slightly.

I took a slow, deep breath and closed my eyes before removing the seal from the flap. What had Louis sent over this time? He was the only person doting on me and sending sweet sentiments of affection and allure. His notes and letters were always so enchanting yet mysterious. I could almost taste the sweetness of his words, the way they danced on my tongue like a delicious confection. They were filled with fondness and longing, leaving a lingering taste of compassion. Words like secret treasures, glinting with hidden meanings that danced on the page like fireflies.

But before I could open the letter, Sandra popped in. Holding a box of donuts as a tempest.

"Did you have a pleasant lunch?"

"Lunch .... umm, it was cozy." The scent of the donuts surrounded my senses and invited me in.

"Have one. They are delicious." She opened the pink box to display the colorful sweet treats. Knowing I did not need the sugar, I took one anyway.

"We have quite the variety today I see." The glazed treat melted in my mouth as Sandra reminded me about the RSVP.

"Don't forget the---" With my hand in the air, I cut her off.

"No worries. I was just thinking about that, sort of." Great!" she winked.

I smiled and waved her off, eager to get back to my surprise of the day. The rhythmic tap of her footsteps faded as she walked away with the office door closing softly behind her.

Alone in the quiet aftermath, the air held a sense of anticipation. It was if the universe itself awaited the unveiling of the unexpected. I swelled with a readiness to open the envelope and dive right into whatever entrancement it contained.

Expecting Louis's usual signature stationary, my eyes were met with a different style and shade of ivory. A yellow card stock with edges slightly bent, as if touched by unseen hands. My fingertips grazed the paper, feeling the slight texture of the paper fibers, like tracing the veins of a leaf, freshly cut from a withering vine.

I stared for a moment, taking in the air of suspense. My fingers brushed against the letter, and began to tremble uncontrollably, a physical manifestation of my growing anxiety. My skin prickled and goosebumps rose on my arms as if a cold hand had brushed against them. The air felt thick and heavy and even the slightest sound seemed amplified.

With zeal, I carefully opened the letter. My eyes studied each letter and syllable. The words whispered across the page stirring a river of orchestrated emotions as I read: "*Out of sight, but not out of mind. You can run darling but, you cannot hide. I am watching you.*"

The letter fell slowly from my fingertips and onto the floor. My tea tipped and spilled all over the vibrant hue of the navy blue folder. The label read: The Monroe Project.

And so— it begins.

About the author

From an early age, Stephanie Tarver knew she wanted to be a published author someday. She developed an adoration for the arts and favored literary fiction. For years, she has admired the works of various fiction and non-fiction giants, all writers of emotionally deep human stories. Stories that inspired Stephanie to fulfill her dreams as a writer and entrepreneur.

She is a successful business owner, devoted mother, and a creative visionary. In addition, Stephanie is an avid reader, publisher, designer, and financial manager. Follow Stephanie on social media for news and updates on her latest book release and tour.

Web: www.stephanietarverbooks.com
Facebook: @authorstephanietarver
Instagram: @steph.tarver